John E. Howard is a husband, father, and grandfather. He is a retired accountant for The General Motors Corporation, an ordained deacon in the Christian Church and a decorated Vietnam veteran. He earned an associate of arts degree in higher accounting at a Dayton business college. He furthered his education though night courses at Wright State University. He is a native of Fairborn, Ohio, but now lives in The Villages, Florida, with his wife, Vicki.

In Appreciation

This book is dedicated to the ladies of my life for their caring presence ever beside me.

Alma – my kind and good mother, Vicki – my wife and true love, April – our precious daughter, Brooke – our sweet granddaughter.

Who can find a virtuous woman? For her price is far above rubies. The heart of her husband doth safely trust in her, so that he shall have no need of spoil. She will do him good and not evil all the days of her life. She seeketh wool, and flax, and worketh willingly with her hands. She is like the merchants, ships; she bringeth her food from afar. She riseth also while it is yet night, and giveth meat to her household, and a portion to her maidens. Prov. 31:10-15

Strength and honor are her clothing; and she shall rejoice in time to come. She opened her mouth with wisdom; and in her tongue is the law of kindness. She looketh well to the ways of her household, and eateth not the bread of idleness. Her children arise up, and call her blessed; her husband also, and he praiseth her. Prov.31:25

"Isn't God great when He asks us just to love like he does?"

John E. Howard

THE DEACON AND THE SHIELD

AUSTIN MACAULEY PUBLISHERS™

LONDON * CAMBRIDGE * NEW YORK * SHARJAH

Ordering Information
Quantity sales: Special discounts are available on quantity purchases by corporations, associations, and others. For details, contact the publisher at the address below.

Publisher's Cataloging-in-Publication data
Howard, John E.
The Deacon and the Shield

ISBN 9781641829793 (Paperback)
ISBN 9781643783970 (Hardback)
ISBN 9781641826464 (ePub e-book)

Library of Congress Control Number: 2021908870

www.austinmacauley.com/us

First Published (2021)
Austin Macauley Publishers LLC
40 Wall Street, 33rd Floor, Suite 3302
New York, NY 10005
USA

mail-usa@austinmacauley.com
+1 (646) 5125767

Preface

As a battlefield soldier that survived the Vietnam War[*], I am honored to introduce a testimonial story that personifies truth about a mental disease that affects so many lives. It's called Post Traumatic Stress Disorder. Unfortunately, many of those suffering go untreated and try to live peacefully with their PTSD affliction and maintain a symbolic way of life. Depicted in this tribute is one such individual that battles his devils while trying to fulfill his duty as an ordained Deacon in the Christian Church. Characters in this heartfelt tale are fictional and any resemblance to any particular person is purely coincidental.

How might one feel emotionally who has PTSD?

Have mercy upon me, O Lord, for I am in trouble: mine eye is consumed with grief, yea my soul and my belly. For my life is spent with grief, and my years with sighing: my strength faileth because of mine iniquity, and my bones are consumed. Psalms 31:9,10

I am forgotten as a dead man out of mind: I am like a broken vessel. Psalms 31:12

What Is PTSD?

Exposure to actual or threatened death, serious injury, or sexual violation.

Directly experience or witness in person to the traumatic events. Learning that the traumatic events occurred to a close family member or close friend which may have been violent or accidental. Constant exposure to traumatic events such as the service of first responders, police and fire departments, medical personnel, and the American combat soldier.

---

[*] Btry. A, 1st Battalion, 14th Artillery, 198th Light Infantry Brigade, Americal Division, Chu Lai, Vietnam. (105mm Howitzer)

Symptoms: Flashbacks or other dissociative reactions in which the individual feels or acts as if the traumatic events are recurring. Distressing dreams in which the content or effect of the dream is related to the traumatic events. Intense or prolonged psychological distress and reactions to reminders of the traumatic events.

How is this affliction apparent to others?

Persistent and exaggerated negative beliefs about himself, others, or the world; such as: I am bad – no one can be trusted – the world is dangerous – distorted blame of self or others and/or fear, horror, or shame – inability to experience positive emotions – estrangement from others – reckless or self-destructive behavior.

Hundreds of thousands of veterans and their families suffer severe psychological and emotional difficulties related to military service. There is no single cure for those afflicted with debilitating, chronic PTSD. It is recognized that continual care to anchor gains in treatment is required. As reported by The Vietnam Veterans of America, they sponsor workshops and town halls that focus on identification and treatments. Discussions deal with recognizing and managing triggers, promoting personal growth and self-care.[*]

Alcohol and other drugs, including prescription drugs, have also had serious impact on the quality of life of veterans and their families. The importance of getting help to someone before they die of their own hand, must be stressed.

Currently, the country of Vietnam has its own PTSD and carries open wounds in the suffering of her children from the remaining environmental and genetic devastation of Agent Orange; a legacy of the Vietnam War.

---

[*] vvaveteran.org publications

Sergeant Eddy Riffle, while serving in The Republic of Vietnam, escaped the fatal grasp of death's collector. But like so many soldiers, Eddy hid his hurt, shame and bitterness of that war within the far-reaches of his mind – not ever forgotten, but stored away. This affliction can last a lifetime and lurks in the dark places of one's soul and waits for the right opportunity to do the most damage. After many years of playing tag with this suppressed sickness, his version of PTSD struck with a vengeance.

Achievements: Husband, father, grandfather, decorated military combat veteran, educated at State College and Law School, attorney-at-law, private investigator, public defender for Orange County, Florida, and church deacon. A successful life? "There is a way which seemeth right unto a man, but the end thereof are the ways of death." Prov. 14:12.

PTSD calamities: Wounding of his soul derived by the harshness of war takes him to a dark place. Through induced weakness, he struggles with right vs wrong – he loses love of family and friends – tainted devotion – stumbles into violent situations – entertains times of instability – yearns for sympathy for his own poor soul – battles himself for self-forgiveness – blindly tries to serve two masters, God or mammon – turns away from the blessings of faith – loses hope and falls to rock bottom where sometimes he is unable to distinguish truth from fantasy.

In his own words: "I'm thinking that all is vanquished, my career, my family, my Christian faith, my reputation, and my happy way of life. I gave it all away through self-indulgence and weakness. Too much! I'm stuck in self-destruction mode with debilitating flashbacks and nightmares – the terror and revenge type. At times, I feel like I'm capable of anything and committing acts that I can't remember or don't want to admit. Questions are swirling in my head with confusing answers. And now my conscience will not turn me loose. I'm just plain afraid of what they will say about me on the judgement day.

What will my family and friends think about me then? And will I hear those thundering words from on high: 'The Deacon lost his way?'"

Someone once said: "The devil loves untold secrets especially those that fester in the darkness of one's soul."

Desperate and with the lust for life almost lost, Eddy Riffle believes that he envisions a visit from the heavenly archangel, St. Michael. Boldly, he challenges the angel with great defiance which convinces the heavenly appearance that the time is not right for collection and grants a reprieve. Within this blessing is an offer of a soul-saving mandate: "The Shield."

Eddy Riffle's story will not end with failure but begins anew. Readers will revel in his recovery and how he returns to God and family, in an emotional roller coaster tale of action, drama, suspense, some light-hearted humor, love, and faith. Please enjoy!

For thou, Lord, wilt bless the righteous; with favor wilt thou compass him as with a shield. Psalms 5:12

Chronology of Events

PART 1

The early years: Deaconship – Drafted into the United States Army – tour of duty in Vietnam – returns to USA, family, and church – Post Traumatic Stress Disorder, PTSD affliction begins – coexists with episodes – over time he becomes an educated, professional man but hides his sickness – allows barrier to God to thicken.

PART 2

History to present time: Serves two masters, God and mammon – gets paid the wages of sin – estranged from family – endures hard times at the bottom – hates his temptress into near disaster – mental affliction worsens – selective memory.

PART 3

The struggle: Believes he is given a vision of St. Michael, the Archangel – receives a reprieve and a mandate – edges into the clutches of The Employer of Bought Souls – a sting operation – a mysterious "sniper" is on the loose – meets Abaddon, the angel of the bottomless pit who is after revenge.

PART 4

Recovery: the true soul emerges on Thanksgiving Day – Father Drake offers help – wrestles St. Michael on Christmas Day – defends in court Triple AAA – returns to family on Valentine's Day, redemption – Easter: St. Gabriel's message/vision of Jesus on the road to Golgotha.

PART 5

Almost there, but: The struggle intensifies: suspected of murder – ambushed by criminal elements/wounded – near death/comatose – has coma induced visions – subpoenaed into court – the sniper is unmasked – Bill (KIA) returns in spirit – PTSD bridled through The Shield.

Finale

St. Michael returns with "The Verdict – Eddy Riffle" via the weighing on the scales – A just weight and balance are the Lord's: all the weights of the bag are his work. Prov.

The Deacon's Homily – The Shield – seek, discover, believe, understand, sanctify.

The Next Word – the future? – "Behold, I send you forth as sheep in the midst of wolves: be ye therefore wise as serpents, and harmless as doves." Matt. 10:16

The Office of a Deacon

As an ordained deacon in the First Church of Christ, my duty is to serve the church and its members in whatever capacity that may be required. In that endeavor, I write this book.

"Likewise, must the deacons be grave, not double-tongued, not given to much wine, not greedy of filthy lucre; holding the mystery of the faith in a pure conscience. And let these also first be proved; then let them use the office of a deacon being found blameless. Even so must their wives be grave, not slanderers, sober, faithful in all things. Let the deacons be the husbands of one wife, ruling their children and their own houses well. For they that have used the office of a deacon well, purchase to themselves a good degree and great boldness in the faith which is in Christ Jesus." 1 Tim. 3:8-13.

Chapter One
"The Soldier – 1967-1968"

Twelve months is a long time in a combat zone when every second could be the last – similar to the Greek proverb: The Sword of Damocles, which epitomized the great fear of having to live with the constant threat of death. A huge and heavy sword was hung above the throne and over the head of Damocles and secured by the single hair of horse's tail to evoke the sense that the fragile hair would inevitably break and thereby render sudden and instant death. Such is the life of the frontline soldier who will experience this non-relenting anxiety in the effort to do his duty.

Sergeant Eddy E. Riffle

When duty calls:

"This charge I commit unto thee, son Timothy, according to the prophecies which went before on thee, that thou by them mightiest war a good warfare; holding faith, and a good conscience; which some having put away concerning faith have made shipwreck." I Tim: 1:18-1.

"Also, I heard the voice of the Lord, saying, whom shall I send, and who will go for us? Then said I, here am I; send me." Isa 6:8

"In other words, keep the faith, obey lawful orders and do your duty, and maintain a good conscience while doing so!"

Eddy Riffle is a Vietnam veteran. It was not a popular war, but it was his war. He answered the call to duty and did what his government asked of him. He had nothing to do with the politics. His family prayed to God for his safe and healthy return. His in-country tour of duty: 12 months. His mission: Obey all lawful orders and stay alive. He was drafted at 22 years of age. He was married at the time. His buddies in the U.S. Army affectionately called him "The Deacon" – a title well earned.

"Hey Bob, I feel like I'm a sitting duck. It's pitch-black and I can't see anything. If they have my forehead as a target, I'll never know what happened. Pop a flare and let's take a look."

(*Poof* – light for several seconds as the flare makes it way downward)

"Eddy, I think I see something, over on the right, by those big clumps of trees. Give them some of that .50-cal!" (*Tat, tat, tat, tat* – about 50 rounds worth)

"Bob, wake up, Bill, I think I hear something like snapping branches and rustling noises. It's coming from over there right where I was firing – sounds to me like a lot of talk going on – getting louder. Hit another flare, quick!"

(*Poof* – light for several seconds as the flare makes it way downward)

Eddy shouts: "Oh no! Here they come – must be a million – they're running right at us. Bill, get the claymores ready! Bob, set off the sirens!"

While the warning alarm was blaring away, Eddy let loose with the .50-cal machine gun and Bob fired his M-16 rifle and Bill triggered the claymore mines – one by one, and as fast as he could. The ordnance burst in every direction around the outside perimeter but it was not enough to deflect the horde of terror. The entire camp was now awakened and alerted and on their way to their assigned positions. Help would soon reach the guard post. Eddy screamed: "They better hurry, we're being overrun!" It didn't help the frantic trio that incoming mortars were now landing too close for comfort. Where would the next one land?

"Hey, Deacon, Eddy, calm down – it's only a dream! You're safe, man! We're on the way home, remember? Look out the window – nothing but blue skies."

"Wow, Bob, I keep having this nightmare, over and over. I know we made it, but in this dream, I'm trapped with no way out of that guard post and they just keep coming and yelling. It's that horrible look on their faces as if they possess no fear and will not stop – never stop! And, I can't forget Bill – how he fought so hard and for so long and then, you know."

Bob tried to help: "It's alright, man – I have them too. It'll get better when we get home to the land of the big PX. I still can't believe we are actually on this plane. It's such a beautiful day to be going home to our wives and moms. No time for bad thoughts – not today!"

"Bob, there's something else that I haven't mentioned before – too scared! It's the way we escaped. Remember when that mortar round hit the bottom of our guard post and it toppled over and crashed – with us still inside. And how we were knocked unconscious. And then we woke up the next morning and everything was over – all the fighting and commotion. Well, here's the weird part: I think I was awake right after the shock. It was like I was half-dead and half-alive. Something or somebody else was there with us. I could not recognize the figure but it was obvious. Whatever it was, it shielded us from the NVA as they paraded around looking for somebody to shoot. They never saw us because this mysterious object deflected their vision by spreading his six big wings that covered us. Then that giant protector waved a great sword that flamed fire and light. It was like sudden encompassing brightness that blinded the attackers and they just stumbled away in other directions. After that, I passed out completely until you shook me back to life. Even now, I believe that an angel saved us and that the vision was not just a figment of my imagination that I conjured in my fright."

"That is weird, Eddy! Better not repeat that story too loud – they might keep you for evaluation or something. Don't let nothing keep you in this man's army any longer than that steak dinner that is waiting for us at Ft. Lewis. But, to ease your thoughts, my mom would believe you in a heartbeat. She told me just before I left that angels have bulletproof wings and if I'm a good boy, will protect me. Maybe she was right."

"Yeah, Bob, probably so. But when I found poor Bill in the rubble, he was barely conscious. I tried to help and prayed with him but I knew that he was already too far gone to save – even for the angels. His last words were of his mother. His last look was a smile. I really hope that figure was truly an angel and it took him away from that awful mess to that better place that awaits us all."

"You are so right, man, but we got to forget for now – let's play 21 to make the time go faster."

After a long flight, the pilot announced: "This is the captain. It's with great pleasure that I am privileged to inform you that you are now in the territory of the United States of America. Look below and you will see the Pacific coastline. It's time to buckle up because we will be landing in about 20 minutes. Welcome to the USA and to Fort Lewis, Washington. And thank you for your service to your country." Then, the entire plane erupted with robust and lingering cheers as a feeling of euphoria swept the embattled veterans who were coming home. "Thank you, God!"

Eddy, at times, did not think that he would make it home in one piece. His fleeting moments of solace only surfaced by visualizing and remembering his lovely wife. But time did pass, every second by second, minute by minute, and finally, here he sits on the plane, safe and alive. But the toll has already been taken. Eddy's spirit was frayed to the last strand and his soul tested to the core. Few people have ever experienced the essence of life where truth is absolute and is not clouded by a phony facade. Eddy and many of his fellow soldiers throughout the ages have lived there. The trip from ground zero back to a USA way of life and how it sometimes can be so frivolous, takes grit – some make it and some can't, and some just don't want to try.

Before Eddy left for that war, he was ordained as a deacon by the "laying on of hands" by the elders. With all the near misses in battle, he felt that he was being watched over – maybe because of that particular blessing. It was during battle action that he earned the title, The Deacon – given to him by his fellow soldiers. His words of prayer before battles and his compassion for the wounded did not go unnoticed and earned respect. Although he was thankful for his personal good luck, he had mixed emotions: "Sometimes it felt right and sometimes it felt selfish." But he always kept one plan of action: "Help my brothers, serve 12 months, go home to sanity and a peaceful and loving existence."

Bob and Eddy went their separate ways but vowed to stay in touch. Maybe someday they will get together, a reunion. But for now, neither are desirous of remembering old times and the events that stained their lives.

Family and friends welcomed Eddy home with that love, support, and understanding, but some citizens of the USA were not so kind. There were open protests with shouts of "baby-killers or murderers." With such hateful scorn, it was trying at times, and even though his goal was in clear sight, it stayed just out of his reach: "Eddy's body was home but his soul was still on the way and searching."

After he calmed down and enjoyed his family surroundings, he resumed a purposeful life at home, at work, and at church with the resumption of his deacon duties. Although the scars and terrible memories will never leave completely, Eddy has learned to coexist. For the individual soldier, there is not much righteousness in war. To survive, things must be done without choice. They are hard to live with. And without public support and understanding, the soldier sometimes will put the blame on himself. His belief about his eternal home is often tarnished into an afterthought and thereby a barrier to God is erected.

Many years have now come and gone for Eddy Riffle and he currently finds himself swimming in awkward situations which this time could prove to be the last straw. He tried hard, really hard, to be the man he envisioned of himself. But that obstruction to God always stood in the path – too thick to break!

And, so it was with Eddy, he lost the strength of family and friends and without hope, he slowly tumbled to a sorry state of despair and loneliness – "The Deacon" faded into submission. Once, through faith and devotion, he served but one master – God. Now, through circumstance and temptation, he serves two masters. The struggle; his sickness begat weakness, which begat temptation, which begat the flourishing toward human desires and greed, which begat his downfall.

No man can serve two masters: for either he will hate the one and love the other; or else he will hold to the one, and despise the other. Ye cannot serve God and mammon, Matt. 6-24

Why Does Mankind Try to Serve Two Masters?

"In the beginning, God created the heavens and the earth. And on the sixth day, God created mankind in his image and named them Adam and Eve. As part of their being, the Creator gave Adam and Eve, and their descendants, the marvelous ability to reproduce eternal souls which was withheld from angels. Because of this, an infuriated and arrogant angel known as Satan, led a force of defiant angels against God and became devoted to the downfall of mankind. To show his anger, the serpent in the Garden of Eden deceived Eve and she then persuaded her husband, Adam, to eat of the forbidden fruit from the tree of knowledge of good and evil.

Because of their disobedience, they were expelled from the Garden of Eden and Adam was given the task of tilling the earth from whence he was taken. Eve was given the task: 'In sorrow thou shalt bring forth children.' Sin and disobedience, originated by the free will of mankind in the Garden of Eden, has manifested itself until this day. 'For dust thou art, and unto dust shalt thou return.'" Gen. 1-4, 19.

What is man that thou art mindful of him? Thou madest him a little lower than the angels; thou crownedst him with glory and honor and didst set him over the works of thy hands: Heb. 2:6-7

From the Author:

Patriotism is the one human emotion that solidifies Americans with spirited resolve to maintain a way of life that was bought and paid for by human lives. The prize: "Equality of justice, freedom for all, and the pursuit of happiness." But the world is constantly changing and many of our forefathers' intended principles are systematically being diminished with new and radical philosophies and lifestyles – thus the fulfillment of Biblical prophesies.

July 4th and Independence Day: "I have a small U.S. flag sticking from my pen and pencil cup, and I put some more flags around the driveway. I attend some of the veterans' activities. I go to the parades and proudly salute the flag. I was an Army artillery soldier and I saw firsthand what brave men and women must achieve to protect and defend the United States of America. Hopefully, the citizens of this country will never lose sight of those sacrifices."

The international conflicts of the past 100 years have redefined the meaning of a soldier's duty: "Doing what it takes and giving of his all – get it done!" In World War II alone, more than 405,000 troops were killed and 670,000 wounded. More than 100 million people from more than 30 countries served, including 16 million from the USA. It resulted in an estimated 50 million fatalities – that's what it took to save humanity from evil.

In Vietnam, more than 58,200 U.S. troops were killed in America's effort to prevent another communist victory after the failed Bay of Pigs Invasion and construction of the Berlin Wall. More than three million Americans served in the war, and 1.5 million saw combat. The United States ended its involvement in 1975 after the fall of Saigon. By that point, military and civilian fatalities were estimated to be between 800,000 and 3.6 million.

Other 20th century wars: World War I, Korean War, and the current War on Terror. Today, many USA combat soldiers (peacemakers) are being asked to fight in the Middle Eastern area and Afghanistan. To be successful, they need their fellow Americans' support and admiration both at home and abroad.

"To everything there is a season, and a time to every purpose under the heaven: A time to kill, and a time to heal. A time of war, and a time of peace." Ecc. 3:1-8.

"Blessed are the peacemakers: for they shall be called the children of God." Matt. 5:9.

From the Author's Personal Experiences:

On March 16, 1968, as a soldier in the US Army, I was treated with a special mission: leave Da Nang, Vietnam, on a commercial airline with a destination of Hawaii. I had earned a 5-day R&R leave of absence. It was there that I would meet my wife, Vicki, for a short rest from the struggles of war. Soldiers in Vietnam were awarded one such "rest and relaxation" trip per year.

Just before arriving in Hawaii, many of my fellow fatigued soldiers eagerly peered out windows hoping to see any appearance of a quiet, peaceful land. A common thirst: relief from the awful noises of Vietnam – gunfire, explosions, rockets, helicopters whirling to and fro, voices screaming missions, and just plain clamor.

Then, a voice: "Anybody know what that long runway that's sticking out and above the waters is being called?"

No response from anyone, so the soldier felt obligated to answer his own question: "It's known as The Wailing Wall."

Looks of puzzlement spread and no one volunteered to reply – everyone was too excited because this plane was about to land and the anticipation of meeting loved ones had taken charge. There were a lot of happy faces so why would we want to spoil the party?

My wife and I enjoyed our short escape from reality by relishing in the fruits of Hawaii – tropical environment with calm breezes, sweet to the taste foods and jovial island entertainment, pig roast, poi and just plain relaxing together. It was as if we were new sweethearts, just married – a real blessing and worth the emotional pain of dreading a soon-to-be parting. The time went too fast and the inevitable arrived – the hard part – six more months of duty lie just ahead – a short trip away. I began worrying about that sword that hung over the head of Damocles and secured by the single hair of a horse's tail. It had to be near the break point! I was only 23 years old and did not want to miss the happiness and excitement that our lives together had promised.

Why was it called The Wailing Wall? Lots of sorrow and crying occurred on that wall – wives refused to let loose and the soldiers didn't want to go back to a mess that was called a war, but they had no choice. Rides back to Vietnam were very quiet and somber. There was nothing to say – just private thoughts.

I was soon back at my post in Chu Lai and was informed about "The My Lai Massacre" – March 16, 1968. For me, the happiness of life was again challenged as I was reminded that life was still being treated as cheap and not revered as a sacred temple. An emotional thought crossed my mind as I strapped on my weapons and gear: "Except for the grace of God, there go I."

A horrific event had occurred. It will not be forgotten and is recorded in the annals of history. The atrocity happened at My Lai – only three miles from a landing zone called Cherry Hill, Chu Lai – my post.

An American United States Army officer was subsequently convicted by court-martial of murdering 22 unarmed South Vietnamese civilians on that March day. This convicted soldier was part of an infantry unit that had been trained in Hawaii and probably not prepared for the mental anguish of war. In the first few months of in-country fighting (some during the Tet Offensive), this unit lost a good portion of their men – KIA or by severe wounds.

The soldier's words at the trial: "I was ordered to go in there (My Lai) and destroy the enemy. That was my job that day. That was the mission that I was given. I carried out the order that I was given. I do not feel wrong in doing so."

By a six-officer jury, the soldier was sentenced to life imprisonment and hard labor at Fort Leavenworth. In a telephone survey, about 80% believed that the sentence was too harsh and that the soldier had been made a scapegoat. After several years in prison and many appeals and trials, the soldier was eventually freed – some 8 years after the My Lai Massacre.

On that storied day, many years ago, a weary soldier probably suffering from mental illness or PTSD, lost the American way of life. The root cause of the incident was the infliction of traumatic events – the kind that a human being cannot forget – not ever. To coexist and in desperation, a victim might drive the horrors of such trauma deep into the dark places of their mind – hoping and praying that it will stay silent forever!

The soldier's words after release: "There is not a day that goes by that I do not feel remorse for what happened. I am very sorry."

The author's observations: After serving two years of active duty, that included a tour in Vietnam, a "US" soldier (draftee) usually was placed on inactive reserve (no meetings or summer camps) for four additional years. This requirement completed the six-year military obligation. However, during those four years, one was subject to being called up for another stint; it was possible but not probable. But the mere thought of being back in Vietnam often caused "our particular soldier" PTSD nightmares. With reenactments of his past events, he became "like that broken vessel."

Sgt. Eddy Riffle's traumatic past flared through nightmares and reenactments that often repeated in various scenarios. He chose to stay silent as possible and bare the emotions upon his own back and suffer the consequences. For some reason, he thought that he was still doing his duty by not talking.

His ghost sleep: "In my dream, I thought that I was home free, but not so! I received a call from Uncle Sam which changed everything. They wanted more troops for Vietnam. There was a shortage of replacements for soldiers that have completed their tours and are returning home – not many re-ups for my PMOS or primary duty classification. So, they notified a large number of battle-tested war veterans to report for active duty and another deployment. I had to go or face the consequences of jail time which would effectively end my self-respect and my place in society."

"I find myself back in Vietnam: It hurt to leave home and family again. I thought that my life ahead would be blessed and full of peace and love. But now I have twelve months to be lucky again and not be in the wrong place at the wrong time. Everybody that serves in Vietnam needs supreme luck because there are no completely safe spots in this whole country."

"So, here I am, getting off the truck at Cherry Hill, Chu Lai." I see one of my buddies from the last tour. But, wait! He was a casualty of war – KIA. He sees me and yells: "Hey, how you doing, Deacon. I thought that you went AWOL and snuck home a few months ago."

"Gordon, is that you? Great to see you again. If I had run off, I wouldn't be here right now. Jail might be better."

Then, I saw another familiar face: "Say, look over there. Isn't that Dietrich?" He was also a casualty of war from my last tour – KIA. Dietrich looks in my direction and waves. "Hey, Deacon, you bum! How did you get here? Are you still preaching?"

"Nah, it's a long story. Just unlucky, I guess. No more preaching for me, nobody will listen anyway. But, tell me: 'Why are you guys still here? I thought, oh well.'"

Gordon speaks: "It's alright to talk about it. We know the score. We were hit and went down. That's the way of war. You know how it is. Can't help it. But, Dietrich and me can't go home just yet. We have some work to do. We go from battle to battle and try to influence where we can. We might nudge someone out of harm's way; that kind of stuff. They can't see us like you can. Why can you see us?"

"I just don't know! Maybe I'm dead too!"

"How do I tell Ellie that I'm walking dead?"

"I must be dreaming. I can't wake up! Wake up – no use!"

"God help me because I hate this place – it makes my body ache!"

My eyes open to the darkness of my bedroom. Ellie is sleeping next to me. It was another nightmare, whew. My first emotion is relief that it was a dream. Then, a sense of euphoria as I realize that I'm still at home and surrounded by love's comfort. Later, the shock hits. The reality of the dream surrounds me and keep me awake and fretful the rest of the night. I don't tell Ellie. The next day I will be hard to live with. My mind can't handle hurtful thoughts about the events that occurred during my year at hell's front door. So, I seek relief through drink and other.

Sunday turned sour: The church was full with a lot of sinners today, but the minister was only talking to me. He seemed to be staring right at my baby-blues and didn't like what he was seeing. I told myself not to blink and don't smile. It's a western showdown, let him draw first. My face wanted to turn away and yield, but I remained strong; no flinching. The minister backed off and dropped his eyes just long enough to snort: "Page 97 and sing like you mean the words."

The audience began singing: "I was lost deep in sin and far from the peaceful shore." They were singing about me. The minister must have told them that I was the wayward sheep of the congregation and it was up to them to drag me from the swirling waters.

I gazed about the spacious worship center. Everybody was looking at me as they sang. Their eyes seemed to be saying: "You poor soul, why are you so weak, be a man and stand up and confess your mischief ways. We know what you did – sinner!"

I stood up alright but they weren't going to intimidate me any longer. I screamed: "You bunch of crybabies. You are always complaining about standing in line, or too much traffic, or someone is in your way. All of you are self-righteous, do-nothings, and don't understand what the edge of life is all about; the truth of it all. You just don't know!"

Ellie stood up beside Eddy and tried to reason with him, but it was not getting through – he was in a trance. It got quiet, really quiet. No one said a word until the minister held up both hands: "Mr. Ripple, what is the matter, are you alright?"

"Yes sir! Outstanding sir! I know what you're going to do! Tonight, you're planning on sending me out on another LRRP mission. This time I won't make it back. Don't you understand. I'm short with only a few days left. I'm going home. Must you do this to me?"

The minister was now wearing a full-bird colonel's uniform; jungle fatigues with cap and insignia. The look on his face typified a condescending officer pretending to console a shell-shocked soldier. "Sgt. Riffle, what is a LRRP mission? Tell this body of loyal patriots what's keeping you from your assigned duty!"

"Long Range Reconnaissance Patrol, sir! As if you didn't know, it's a dark and dangerous trek through bush, vines, and skeeters. It's enemy territory all the way with gooks hiding everywhere, or two-step snakes – or worse; booby traps. Sometimes we don't come back. Some of us are never found. To stay alive, we have to do things. I can't take it anymore. But you war-mongers don't care. You are heartless. Like all the other desk-sitters, you hold meetings. You live frivolous lives with authority to blame the whole mess on little old me. I've had just about enough of this war and I'm going to – a sudden and startling wake up!"

Eddy quickly opens his sore and frantic eyes: "Where am I?"

He had no clue about his circumstances, but just looking around the room brought him back to consciousness. He was in the Emergency Room! "What have I done?"

Ellie stood nearby but was leaning on a chair. She looked scared while talking to a doctor! "He hasn't done this lately. It seems that he just goes back to the jungles. That's where his nightmares live. I thought that he was better, but he can't forget or forgive. It's stuck in his mind, somewhere. I'm more than just being worried. This episode was the worst. What I could tell, he was fighting himself while in church; his good versus his bad. He almost went into a fit of terror."

Mumbling: "I'm sorry Ellie. I don't know what happened. Something came over me that I had no control – hope I didn't hurt anyone. So sorry."

After tests and examinations, nothing could be pinpointed except mental induced trauma and a return of PTSD. Something triggers these episodes. What is it that seeps into the dark places of his mind and wrenches hurtful memories free – to explode?

Medicines didn't help, but it made everybody feel better that it might. Eddy played along, but inside he felt that it was hopeless and therefore refused further treatments. His position: Nothing will change his past where he experienced many sorrowful things and some of them were of his own choosing. He has no excuse for himself. It's all there on his permanent record.

Church folks were aware of Eddy's sickness and tried to help. They understood his condition and deemed it the proper thing for Eddy to continue his deaconship. He agreed with the church board and resumed his duties like collecting the offering, calling on the sick, maintenance of the building, delivering communion to the shut-ins and serving on the church board. He even taught Sunday School.

Over the years, Eddy buried himself in his work profession and became a success. He and Ellie also became the proud parents of twin daughters which he loved dearly. His PTSD went into relative submission. But, even with all this effort, something was just not right. His conscience was not healed, but instead lurked beneath the surface, waiting for the first sign of weakness.

Chapter Two

"The Wages of Sin"

This "wages of sin" chapter is revealed by his own lips and brings the reader up to date on his life, achievements, failures, and his chilling mental state. Disaster is near!

So, I played with matches and got burnt. I willingly allowed myself to be compromised by playful teasing and for my trouble, I was paid "the wages of sin."

The History of Present Time:

My name is Eddy Edward Riffle, but most people just call me Eddy – some used to call me The Deacon, but not lately. Florida, my home, known as the sunshine state, attracts millions of fun-seekers from around the globe every day. It's a perfect place to sneak in a few sins, commit crimes, or even a murder! Some get caught, some don't. I work for the ones that do.

After my service in the Vietnam War, and on the GI Bill and Uncle Sam's student loan program, I graduated from State University. A few years later, I graduated from Law College. My current life: "Attorney at Law, Private Investigator, Public Defender – Orange County."

I perform my services for one thing: "I do this for money – as much as I can get. I don't care if they are guilty or not." I'm not at all particular about my clientele because I play it smart. I always stay at least two steps ahead of my clients and their activity – as I said: I just want their money! If I sound like I'm too big for my pants, you're right. That's my modus operandi and I've still got some room in those extra-large-triple-wide britches!

Personally, I was doing well: Ellie and I were happy – she's a beautiful lady. And, somehow with her, I fathered twin daughters, Lynn and Niki – both now happily married – and I have two grandkids: Jamie and Aaron. Both of their dads, my sons-in-law, served their country in Afghanistan. Then, there's that very nice career that I had in a very successful law firm in Tampa, Florida. 'Had' is a big word!

My relationship with my family was like all middle-class Americans – worked hard and enjoyed the weekends. I often ask myself, "What went wrong?" But then I know the answer – It's in the back of my mind and eats at me! I'm estranged from my wife and children because I cheated. I pretty much am a dirty no-good rat that has a license to associate with other dirty no-good rats – that's what keeps me going! I thrive on being with people who are in sorry shape because my life is not much different than theirs and not an example for others to follow – filled with much regret.

Everything was going my way and my reputation was blossoming. The partners of the firm projected huge plans for me and gave me some of the headline cases. I didn't disappoint them and I was pulling in mega-bucks for the firm and myself. But, like all numbskulls, I let myself be suckered into a mess that derailed everything.

It all started when I put a gag on my personal code of integrity and soothed my conscience by telling that watchdog: "It's alright, Eddy. What's a little fun going to hurt? I won't go too far or venture too much. Besides, everybody is doing it these days, so why not me? Nobody will know – it's all a secret." It began with my fooling around with the girls in the office staff – nothing too bad, but wrong. Small stuff usually leads to large stuff. So, I played with matches and got burnt. I willingly allowed myself to be compromised by playful teasing and for my trouble, I was paid "the wages of sin." And to boot, my episodes returned with a vengeance.

Aebra Ann Arlington (triple AAA – Amorous, Alluring, Attack) is her name and climbing the ladder to success was her game. She possesses the intelligence and savvy required to have easily "someday" made it all the way to the top of our law firm, but she had no intentions of waiting on someday. Her age was pulling forty and for her, it was now or never. I was in her way and had to be eliminated. It was an easy task because I was an easy mark. I've always believed that people are inherently good and because of that misconception, I could not see the worst coming out of Aebra. She reported to me and that made it harassment. "Also, I'm old enough to be her father!"

You've heard it all before: Man takes for granted his happy family life, lets his guard down because of temptation, then makes big mistakes that can't be undone. Aebra set me up with after-work drinks in her office and laughing that was supposed to be rewinding time. It was an innocent time for one of us but I became my own worst enemy and caused my own downfall. I allowed myself to think about "adulterous" scenarios with Aebra. I allowed weakness to flourish. As a result, I was easily tempted and fell prey to her tantalizing taunts.

It happened after a hard day. One too many. She had me by the hand leading me through the door to the copy room. Clothes began flying and things began falling. My conscience became conflicted and began to scream at me. I began thinking about what was happening and how much I could "not" do this. I fought hard to resist and at the last moment, I regained my senses. "Stop!" I shouted.

As if this activity was her devious plan, Aebra rushed out of the copy room while trying to hide her top with previously discarded clothing. And to make things worse, she was now sobbing uncontrollably and yelling that she was being attacked and needed help. "Man, was my face red!"

Here I was, Mr. Dope, shirt off, tie lying in the trashcan, lipstick smeared on my neck, and two wide-open eyes that had "guilty-as-hell" etched right in the pupils. I was a dead duck with no way out. My appeals that nothing seriously happened fell on deaf ears.

Aebra got her way. The partners and Aebra agreed not to press charges. And, the entire incident, my alleged physical attack, would be pushed aside under the legal rug if I would quietly leave the firm with no fuss. In return, I would not be disbarred or publicly embarrassed and I could continue my law career unimpeded. I had to submit.

As you would expect, my home front was devastated and I was banished. I had no place to go except to a seedy motel. Luckily, that only lasted a short time and I located an office in downtown Orlando that contained a suitable back room for a bum like me. That was some time ago and since then I have used my law degree and my experience in the courts to slowly command my own legal services office. With no income-producing clients to start, I had to take gigs as a private investigator, so I could pay the bills for myself and for my family. In a short time by dealing with low-class criminals, I allowed myself to become a low-class jerk and I lost my sympathy toward others.

I tried a few times to explain to Ellie and my family that I was guilty only to a point: "I came to my senses and knew I was doing wrong and did not allow things to progress to the actual act." But the Bible overrules babble: "If you think or lust about doing an act, you are just as guilty as if you really committed that act." So, I'm guilty that I did wrong and accept my punishment. But I will never accept losing my family's love – with it, I lost my self-esteem – once again – this time for all the wrong reasons.

My Mental State:

"My sickness has worsened and I'm plagued with dreams of post-war guilt, general unworthiness, and being a failure to my family. I'm haunted into submission. Too much! I'm now stuck in self-destruction mode and all I think about is mischief and a quick buck. And I can't control my hate and desire for hurt aimed at the 'lady of my weakness – Triple AAA.' Questions are swirling in my head with confusing answers. I need help, but from where?"

"I'm so weak and discouraged that: 'Sometimes I wish.........!'"

For the record, I know what I was taught:

"But I say unto you, that whosoever looketh on a woman to lust after her hath committed adultery with her already in his heart." Matt. 5:28.

"With her much fair speech she caused him to yield, with the flattering of her lips she forced him. He goeth after her straight-way, as an ox goeth to the slaughter, or as a fool to the correction of the stocks." Prov. 7:21-22.

"Let not thine heart decline to her ways, go not astray in her paths. For she hath cast down many wounded: yea, many strong men have been slain by her." Prov. 7:25-26.

"Lust not after her beauty in thine heart; neither let her take thee with her eyelids." Prov. 6:25.

"Disaster Is Near"

Aebra Arlington arrives home. It's late Friday evening after the usual gathering at the pub. She pulls into the driveway. The garage door opens. The luxury model vehicle moves into the garage. The door slowly closes. She is safe.

Behind the shrubs, beside the garage, lurks a masked dark-clad man who has a military-issue bayonet in his right hand. He is breathing hard and fast. He is sweating. His heart is racing. His eyes are fixed with purpose – his hand begins to wave that deadly weapon – a sign that he wants to kill Aebra Arlington. Why? He hates her!

The man becomes stoical. Visions of hand-to-hand combat flash across his mind. Mentally, he is transported back to the Vietnam jungles where that bayonet was sometimes his only defense. He slashes at the bushes while envisioning images of attacking Cong. He trips the security system. Lights and sirens erupt. Off he runs.

Violently, the sweat-soaked man awakens and finds himself at home in his own bed. Another awful nightmare. This has happened before. Each time it gets closer to completion – kill her! The man realizes that he must control his desire for bloodshed aimed at this person that caused his downfall. Her deceit and treachery have left him teetering as if he was standing on the edge of a bottomless pit. To fall from that ledge is forever.

The man mumbles, barely coherent, as he strives to awakens from his trance: "I don't want to hurt anybody – I want to feel good again – It was mostly my fault – I was the aggressor – I have to admit my guilt – if my ego will let me – I have to quit lying to myself – I might do something bad if I don't. I'm The Deacon, so I have to get hold of myself. I'm not this person that I see in the mirror. I can change. I will change. I need love in my life, not hate and vengeance. Ellie, I need you – don't stay away any longer – forgive me."

Was this just another sickness-induced episode? That's what the man had himself believing until: "Under his pillow, he discovered a face mask. Under his bed, a bayonet – Oh no!" The man will seek help from a head-shrink – or so he tells himself – or so he will keep crying himself to sleep.

Chapter Three

"It's Hard Times at the Bottom"

Eddy Riffle, an eternal spirit housed in a human body, is subject to all the temptations and sin that Satan is able to create.

At the same time, mankind is called to "submit to all things which the Lord seeth fit to inflict upon him, even as a child doth submit to his father." "Mosiah 3"

At some point in life, one might be tempted to call out as Jesus did on the cross in the book of Matthew: "My God, my God, why hast thou forsaken me?"

In this chapter, Eddy is about there!

Oh, what peace of mind we often forfeit. Oh, what needless pain we often bear!

Orange County, Florida, City Building, Courthouse

The door opens: "All stand! The Honorable Judge Grace R. Rule, presiding!"

"Eddy, Eddy, wake up, you need to stand for the judge."

"I'll do my best, but it won't be easy. I'm still groggy. Will this take long? Sorry, but it must have been something I ate or drank – or one of my dreams."

Judge Rule: "Mr. Eddy E. Riffle, according to your arrest report, you seem to have lost your way last night. It says here that you were found wandering along Magnolia Street at three o' clock in the morning. And you could not remember where you had been, where you were, or where you were going. You also tested positive for being under the influence. On your behalf, you cooperated with the officer and you were polite. You further stated that you were suffering from a bad case of something or other and it made you stagger and slur words. In consideration of your stated innocence and whining, I will overlook the obvious. Instead, I will consider that you are a licensed attorney that has previously defended your clients in my court and in doing so, reflected professionalism in those proceedings. Before I pass judgment, let me hear your arguments and what you have to say about this arrest and about your general demeanor at such an early hour. By this stage in your life, I'd think you would know better!"

"Sorry, Judge Rule, I am unable to remember much. I wasn't very happy with myself last evening. As you already know, I recently was successful in defending the Malinski Brothers of city corruption, lewd business endeavors, and bribery charges. I can't go into any details, by law, but I will say that the life I'm living is not the life I want, and I'm distressed. The Malinskis threw a big victory party with all the trimmings. Also, there were friendly females there and that's the last I remember. That's about it, your Honor, except to say that it was all a mistake – the whole thing including the case. That's the truth of it."

Eddy did not mention to the judge that he had been having flashbacks and nightmares of post-war trauma that induced his ill-mannered behavior, forgetfulness, and left him distraught and unstable. Such would not be good for a defense lawyer that could not control himself physically or mentally. If this condition surfaced, he would face being disbarred for being unable to be ethically professional!

Unaware of Eddy's sickness, the judge continues: "Mr. Riffle, because of your past standing with this court, and the fact that I am inclined to be lenient in this case, I am giving you 'extenuating circumstances' instead of finding you guilty of being publicly sick with your something. However, you will be 'on notice' with me and I expect you to serve this court as the Public Defender for Orange County until I say different. Do you accept my parameters?"

"I do, your Honor, and thank you!"

"Mr. Riffle, I accept your commitment and I now appoint you as the Public Defender for Orange County – effective as of this date. And as a warning, I know that you are doing some private investigating work, so be careful not to cross any lines. You are on probation with a judge who might not be too sympathetic the next time. If you are having some sort of problem, fix it!"

The gavel: "All stand! – The Honorable Judge Grace R. Rule, court dismissed."

As Eddy left the courthouse, a neatly dressed man followed him: "Mr. Riffle, let me indulge by giving you my card. I'm in need of your services. Call if you are interested. The job is open for a few days. It pays well." After handing Eddy his card, the gentleman fled away hurriedly without waiting for a response.

From the Author:
Conflict within the human spirit is ever-present and unrelenting. The willpower to follow what we know is right, constantly struggles with the willpower to follow the satisfaction of human desires and cravings. And just like Eddy, all of mankind must face the same dilemmas with their free-will ability that is part of their creation.

After all, we're just common everyday people trying to live our lives as best as we can. Some live healthy lives. Some live with disabilities. We try to do our upmost to take care of our loved ones. We do good to others when the occasion arises, and we are able. We get sick physically and mentally. Sometimes we get better, sometimes we don't. We have limitations that try our souls. We feel hurt when other people suffer and die. We mean well when trying to help but often it comes out wrong. We are weak and do wrong things due to temptations. We are strong and do right things due to determination. We hate and we love. We fight and we cherish peace. We are sympathetic and we are selfish. We are benevolent and we are thoughtless. We work hard and obey the laws of the land. We cheat and steal and go to jail. We pay our taxes. We lie on the amount to pay. We pray for health, happiness, substance, peace of mind and forgiveness. Sometimes we recognize that prayers were answered and blessings were bestowed. Sometimes we don't recognize them and are not thankful. After all, we're just human.

Out of the same mouth proceedeth blessings and cursing. My brethren, these things ought not so to be. James 3

Biblical Scriptures are very clear that mankind will someday face a judgment, so how should mankind monitor himself and weigh his own deeds? How will St. Michael, the archangel and guardian of the church, view the different levels of right when he weighs souls and their accomplishments on his scales? And, to what extent will such discernment affect the etching of names in the Book of Life?

Chapter Four

"The Employer of Bought Souls"

In this chapter, we are introduced to the fallen angel of the bottomless pit, Abaddon, a.k.a., The Employer of Bought Souls, who is connected to all the wrong people and isn't to be messed with or denied. "If you know too much, you face a lit fuse. Hold that firecracker in your hand a bit too long and ouch!"

"And they had a king over them, which is the angel of the bottomless pit, whose name in the Hebrew tongue is Abaddon, but in the Greek tongue hath his name Apollyon." Rev. 9:11.

After several sick days of recuperation from that bad case of flu, Eddy was again sober and in need of some ready cash. Bills were stacked high on his desk, school fees were due, and his bookie was calling for payment. Eddy needed to get it in gear! "Somewhere in this mess is a card from that affluent client-on-the-street. Today is Halloween Eve, so why not scare myself up some business?"

Eddy contacted the mystery man, Mr. Client. He accepted the case while ignoring the omen of bad luck; it was afterall, Halloween Day. So, he was now on duty: It was almost midnight and Eddy was awaiting his target. Slowly down the street motored a black luxury model sedan with windows dark. The driver of the vehicle knew exactly where he wanted to go but was being cautious and timely about getting there. To the culprit, this was old hat, and had worked many times before, so there was no reason for him to be apprehensive – just business as usual But, to look in holiday attire and to subvert a chance meeting with authorities, he wore a vampire mask. What better alibi than: "hey, I'm just on my way to a spooky party!"

Eddy's case: Prove that the suspect, one Mr. P. Macks, a successful architect and businessman, used his real estate construction company as a front to gather secret information from his very wealthy clients to burglarize their estates. His method: mechanically draw the blueprints of the estate with a secret passage-way and make it look like an ordinary fabrication schematic. A simple coping saw in the right spot and any doting intruder would have an easy entrance into the den area and right next to the safe that was designed to look well-hidden within the wall. With prior information and knowledge of the exact weight of the safe, it could be easily removed. And, with the twist of a few convenient screws, it's just a matter of lift, tuck, and run – remember to say on the way out: "Good bye and thank you!"

The mistake: Mr. Client specified on his data worksheets his occupation: "Business Investor and Entrepreneur." But what was not listed was the fact that he was also an architect by college degree. And to his trained eye, when he inspected the final build to the blueprint drawings of the estate, he immediately recognized that there had been constructed an easy way for anyone to break into his residence and then steal him blind.

Mr. Client: "I knew I should have designed this place myself, but I was just too busy! So, I'll settle with: Ah ha, you snake in the grass, gotcha." Memo: "Today's crime families get retribution for such encroachments on their turf by the vigilante style: 'hang 'em high!'"

Further: Mr. Client does not have much of a conscience or a tender heart because he obtained his monetary riches by the act of "selling his very soul" to an underworld mob-boss that associates fear. They call him: "The Employer of Bought Souls" – Mr. A. Baddon!

As a good soldier would do, he developed a plan that would keep the family business out of the police spotlight. Decision: Hire an unsuspecting private investigator and let him take all the risk. Then, after he apprehended that rum-bum, justice could be meted in the usual appropriate manner – a proposal – one the crook could not refuse: "Cut a deal and get rich or get a neck-tie party!" The Employer wanted to buy the soul of Mr. Macks – not kill him! A dead man cannot be tempted and is absolutely of no use!

As for an unsuspecting private detective, enter Eddy Riffle. After checking sources on the street, Mr. Client determined that Eddy had the right kind of reputation: "shady." And, after finding out that this PI's residence was at the time, the city jail – that made it even better. So, that's how and why Eddy is now sitting in his car with field glasses in hand – lurking like some common peeping Tom. But to be inconspicuous, he wore an old Lone Ranger mask to appear that he was also just a party guest. Good thinking!

Back to the case: The sedan slowed as it passed the client's estate. It was a big place with an iron gate and security cameras that gave an impression: "Don't do it!" Almost stopping, the sedan cautiously eased around the next corner and into a dark dead-end spot which provided easy entry to the back of the estate.

Witnessing this activity, Eddy moved to a secure spot where he could follow the movement of the potential intruder. The figure of a hooded vampire-man dressed in all black exited the sedan, made his way to the back section, and then climbed over a chain-link fence that was out of eyeshot of the cameras. He moved quick as a house-cat as he raced to the entry point. He carried with him a coping saw, pen light, and one screw driver – all that's required to take another's precious and treasured valuables. "That worm!"

That was all Eddy needed to see. It was definitely the villain that he was hired to apprehend so he hurriedly followed a practiced-pathway into the estate and through an unlocked front door. He then located the den and positioned himself beneath the safe. He pulled his pistol and unlocked the safety. Everything was going as planned. The client had been sent upstairs and told to call 911, and then he was to hide in the closet with his wife. If the police got there in time then Eddy would not have to act and the police could handle the arrest.

Trying to hold his breath, Eddy could hear the wallboard being sawed. The sound stopped. A gentle push and an entryway into the den. A man slid through. With screwdriver in hand, he made his way toward the safe. He flicked on the pen light. He focused on the picture that covered the safe that was hidden within the wall. He removed the picture. He stumbled onto something that felt like a foot. He looked down. There was Eddy with his .45-cal. military-issue pistol in hand and pointing at the man's chest. "Talk about a shock!"

Eddy stood up and reached to unhood the intruder. "Let's see what we have here!" The crook saw his chance and surprised Eddy and unleashed a karate move that sent him spiraling over some fake bushes that sat near the corner of the room. This made Eddy a tad upset so he retaliated with his own form of karate or jungle fighting – crude but effective. He connected and knocked that obnoxious ninja over a few lamps and some other stuff on "his" backward tumble. "Didn't feel so good, did it?"

More wrestling and throwing of bodies ensued and Eddy got downright mad and lost his cool – his hands began to twitch. He managed to locate his 45 lying under a broken vase. A bullet was already chambered, the hammer was cocked, and Eddy's finger was now on the trigger. All four hands were on the pistol struggling for control. A round went off into the wall. More struggling until Eddy prevailed when he was able to place the pistol right between the thief's eyes. By this time, Eddy had worked up a lather. His face was flush with anger and his past military survival training implored him: "Pull the trigger!"

Eddy could not explain to himself what it was that stopped him from that deadly intention. Maybe it was the pleading eyes of the man lying beneath him.

Maybe it was the memory of what killing had done to his soul. Maybe it was his guardian angel. One thing's for sure: Both men were very relieved when Eddy moved safely away even though that pointing 45 was still menacing – one false move and it's trigger-time!

After a few more minutes of getting verbally acquainted, the bare-faced burglar (indeed it was Mr. Macks) sat handcuffed to the desk while supporting a black eye, a red nose, and a hanging, ripped-to-shreds, vampire mask. And, the scumbag was of no mind to associate any further with his captor, whose mask was still on straight. The twist: What seemed like a successful end to another case with a ride off into the sunset, took a turn that totally surprised Eddy. "It was not in the contract!"

Abruptly, the door to the den slammed open and in walked Mr. Client. He was accompanied by several hulking men who had their own pointing pistols. Without saying a word or checking with Eddy, the men went to work and grabbed Mr. Macks by the lapels. They lifted him up and took him and threw him viciously into a waiting van. Apparently, 911 was never called or needed – they use their own protection.

Mr. Client: "Eddy, take off that stupid mask! But, let me say, you did a fantastic job and my boss is very appreciative. He personally witnessed the whole escapade on our secret video system and after you apprehended that burglar, he just smiled and said: 'Riffle's our man – even if he didn't murder the bum.' So, don't be personally concerned about this stooge that you just corralled. We will take care of Mr. Macks. Further, do not call or inform the police about anything that has happened here. Is this all clear? There is no alternative: 'The Employer does not possess forgiving skills in his repertoire!'"

"Yea, it's really clear. I can keep my trap shut."

Mr. Client: "As an incentive, flatfoot, here's a little bonus for you – it's from the man – a check for $15,000. He wrote it out personally. Money is not an object for him. Also, you will get your normal contract amount in the mail and that's a decent payday for a gumshoe. 'The Employer' said to tell you that we will be calling on you in the future when we need a mouth-piece for legal things – don't say yes to him if you ain't man enough!"

Eddy cleared his voice and said: "Why do you call him 'The Employer' and how will I know if he calls?"

"That's his passion! He employs bought souls to carry out his desires, but only with their complete agreement. The rest is not for you to understand right now. He will let you know what is required, if and when. Go back to your normal work routine and be patient – profitable business is in your future if you cooperate 100%.”

Eddy was now very curious and just had to make a statement.: “By the way, Bub (to show his lack of intimidation), why do they call you Mr. Client? I never heard that moniker before. Anything special?”

“That name was given to me by The Employer and that’s good enough for the kind of business I have to accomplish. You see, I was his best customer. And, not only that, ‘Bub’ was already taken by someone that you don’t want to tangle with. So, if you happen to meet him, call him Mr. Bub!”

After discussing a few details of their arrangement, the meeting was concluded and Eddy returned to his office. A few days passed. He was contacted by Mr. Client and given some minor legal matters. Eddy was kept on the outside and looking in while waiting for the meat and potatoes to arrive from the other end of the table. Eddy was pre-warned about getting into deep waters, to wit: “The boss has plenty of smart guys loafing around on his payroll. And, for those that don’t stay loyal or squeal, will get to know those smart guys personally.” Eddy got their message!

Eddy needed to make a demand: “This agreement must be kept under wraps because it would not look favorable for the Public Defender of Orange County to be on the payroll of a notorious capo – I’m no good if I’m doing a stretch!”

Eddy’s personal thoughts: “Why have I been accepted into their confidence and I’ve never laid eyes on the capo. This never happens, even for lifetime gang members. Wonder what he wants of me? I better keep my eyes open wide and my antennas out because something might be cooking in the pot. I might be the ham bone that’s up for bids. And, if Judge G.R. Rule finds out about this, I’m a jail-bird – after she plucks my feathers!”

From the Author: Who is Abaddon and what does he want?

Abaddon, the devil's chief fallen angel of the bottomless pit, is now determined to take an active role by stirring the pot. He will spare no temptation in his quest to convince human eternal spirits to turn away from their Christian beliefs. Eddy Riffle has become his present number-one prime target because he is teetering on the brink while suffering from PTSD and can fall any which way the breeze blows. All he needs is a push. Deception and trickery come in many forms and is a favorite device to entrap the sick, the weak, the unsure, and the lukewarm.

Scripture reference: But there were *false prophets* also among the people, even as there shall be false teachers among you, who privily shall bring in damnable heresies, even denying the Lord that bought them, and bring upon themselves swift destruction. And *many shall follow their pernicious ways*; by reason of whom the way of truth shall be evil spoken of. And shall receive the reward of unrighteousness, as they that count it pleasure to riot in the day time.

"Angel – A Heavenly Messenger"

Basic information about the presence of angels:

In the New Testament, angels are described as being everywhere and as intermediaries between God and man.

"And seeth two angels in white sitting, the one at the head, and the other at the feet, where the body of Jesus had lain." John 20:12.

"Neither can they die any more: for they are equal unto the angels; and are the children of God, being the children of the resurrection." St. Luke 20:36.

"See that you despise not one of these little ones: for I say to you, that their angels in heaven always see the face of my Father who is in heaven." Matt. 18:10.

"Be not forgetful to entertain strangers: for thereby some have entertained angels unawares." Heb. 13:2.

"And Stephen, full of faith and power, did great wonders and miracles among the people. And all that sat in the council, looking steadfastly on him, saw his face as it had been the face of an angel." Acts: 6:15-18.

"For if God spared not the angels that sinned, but cast them down to hell, and delivered them unto chains of darkness, to be reserved unto judgment." 2 Peter 2:4.

How many angels?

"And I beheld, and I heard the voice of many angels round about the throne and the beasts and the elders: and the number of them was ten thousand times ten thousand, and thousands of thousands." Rev. 5-11

$(10{,}000 \times 10{,}000 = 100$ million$) + 1000$s of 1000s or too many to count!

Chapter Five

Archangel – St. Michael

Furrowing his brow, the bully spoke sharply: "I don't need substance and I don't have patience! I'm on a mission. Are you ready?" The visitor then reached out his hand as to shake mine. I paused and pushed back in my chair. I was concerned about his motive and about that menacing sword with the hypnotic glowing tip because it appeared eager to strike.

"Archangel St. Michael"

Information about St Michael:

Michael means "who is like God." He appears to be the one to do battle against Satan and his band of fallen angels. He was chosen to be the chief of all angels and called an Archangel. He is also known as the good Angel of Death and also known as the Grim Reaper. Some religions in the world believe that Michael causes people's death by coming to collect them and carries their soul to Heaven. Also, in the Roman Catholic teachings, St. Michael has four main roles. His first role is as the leader of the Army of God and the leader of heaven's forces in their triumph over the powers of hell. The second and third roles of Michael deal with death. In his second role, he descends at the hour of death and gives each soul the chance to redeem itself before passing; thus, consternating the devil and his minions. In his third role, he weighs souls on his perfectly balanced scales. In his fourth role, Michael is also the guardian of the church.

"And when he had opened the third seal, I heard the third beast say, Come and see. And I beheld, and lo a black horse; and he that sat upon him had a pair of balances in his hand." Rev 6:5.

"And it came to pass that night, that the angel of the Lord went out, and smote in the camp of the Assyrians an hundred fourscore and five thousand: and when they arose early in the morning, behold they were all dead corpses." 11 Kings 19:35

Eddy Riffle's lukewarm Christian beliefs are not strong enough to deter Abaddon's presence and temptations. He has lost the love of his family and respect from his friends. He considers his own situation to be hopeless with no escape. He will not ask God for forgiveness and understanding and therefore is unable to repent. And, he refuses to forgive himself!

God Works in Mysterious Ways, His Wonders to Perform.

Enter St. Michael:

"A precious soul is hanging in eternal balance. As the guardian of the church, I must go. Either I appear as the Grim Reaper and collect his weary soul or I appear as the archangel of God in a vision to Eddy Riffle. I must look into his eyes and reach into his soul to find answers. Then, as it is with all human spirits through their own free-will, he, himself, will navigate his course."

St. Michael kneels before he mounts his black horse: "Being lukewarm is failure and I pray that Eddy Riffle's heart is not penetrated with wickedness but only clouded by forgivable transgressions that he is able to overcome."

The angel then mounts his black horse for the journey to earth. For this heavenly visit, he dresses in golden attire and carries with him the instruments of justice and collection: the weighing scales and the flaming sword of death.

Off to Earth!

I was tired, double-dog tired. But I felt good because Bub (Mr. Client) just gave me a bonus. I sat back in my lousy rocking chair and took a deep breath. There I was in my cramped and stuffy office holding that much needed last pay check up to the light to read the numbers again for the fifth time – $15,000! I put my coffee cup to my lips for a sip when the door to my office squeaked open. I didn't particularly want any more business, but I did need the cash – you can never get enough. My back was to the door and I was too engrossed to immediately turn around. Greetings would have to wait.

A gruff voice: "So, they call you Eddy!"

"So, they call you Eddy!" the visitor repeated himself because I was still paying little attention to him. Visions of myself lying on the beach with a fruit and cola (ha ha) in my hand had all my thoughts. "I need a vacation!"

"That's right, mister," I muttered as I continued to gaze lovingly at the check and salivating about what it could mean. "It's fifteen large and I have a lot of plans for this baby. I'm on my way to Hawaii. The kids need shoes. You know, that kind of stuff."

"You seem sure of yourself," the visitor commented.

This time it caught me like a jab to the nose. There was something about the voice that got my attention. As I turned to meet the visitor, I felt uneasy and apprehensive. To me, the voice was like a bass singer whispering through a megaphone. It was the kind of voice that you only hear in the creepy movies. And, he looked just like me – "what the?"

So, there it stood, beside my desk and dressed in colors of gold from its fancy wraps to ancient-type footwear. And very noticeable was its flowing cape that hid large bulging shoulder pads or something else very large that I could not discern. I immediately jumped to an oddball conclusion. My very own conscience has rebelled and it's facing me for a showdown. "No way!" I whispered.

"How can I help you?" I said with a nervous tone that invited my upper lip to twitch.

"I'm here for business!" it blurted.

I thought: "If it isn't my conscience, who is it?"

I rubbed my eyes and my temples hoping this image was a mirage and it would disappear. It wasn't and it didn't!

My first take: On this man's face there were no happy wrinkles on his cheekbones, like he never smiled, not ever. He looked to me like he was dead serious! And, to increase my alarm, he had an Arab-type sword which fit comfortably in his left hand and it had a shiny tip that drew my eyes and would not let loose. I felt trapped and under its influence. Trying to cool the situation, I offered the visitor some coffee and asked: "What's the sword all about? We're all friends here, aren't we?"

Furrowing his brow, the bully spoke sharply: "I'm the boss-man here and I don't need substance and I don't have patience! I'm on a mission. Are you ready?"

The visitor then reached out his hand as to shake mine or maybe it was a vice-grip to restrain an unwilling participant. I paused and pushed back in my chair trying to elude his hand. I was concerned about his motive and about that menacing sword with the hypnotic glowing tip because it appeared eager to strike.

The visitor glared at me with his piercing eyes! At this point, I became irritated at his aggressiveness and he ticked me off. So, instead of reaching for his outstretched hand, I fumbled for my .45-caliber pistol that was nestled in my waistline. I was ready to shoot this loudmouth if he drew back that sword. If he was here to get me then I would beat him to the punch. My hand grasped for the handle of the .45 but I could not untangle it from my belt. It was no use because the blasted thing would not release. I had no choice but to refold my hands upon the desktop and look stupid and without reaching to shake his hand. The visitor surprisingly was not ruffled in the slightest by my actions nor did he question me about my stubbornness. I told myself, "Get a grip, you wimp!"

The stranger spoke: "Are you done, Mr. Riffle?" He paused for a moment and then he pulled back his hand and covered his sword back into its sheath. "Don't worry about this sword – It has a mind of its own, sometimes. With the turbulent times on earth, it has been busy and needs to be reminded to take a break and rest its hypnotic beam of light."

"Yes, I'm done," I said. "But, what exactly do you want of me and what do they call you anyway? But first, let's be clear about who you are addressing, I'm an attorney and a private investigator licensed by the state of Florida. If you've got business with me, then let's get at it and quit horsing around. I'm in a good mood today with fifteen grand itching my palms, so don't ruin it for me."

From under his cloak, the mysterious illusionist then pulled out something new: "weighing scales." He slapped them down in front of me on my desk. Then he asked me the big question: "Are you afraid of the Judgment Day and if your name is in the Book of Life and what these scales will reveal? These scales operate by their own merit and are not a respecter of persons. Deeds are deeds. What the scales reveal is not biased."

I was somewhat sarcastic when I answered but I was taken back by his brashness. And, what right did he have to ask me those questions in the first place? So, I let him have my answer like Bogie would and with both barrels: "It's a tough world out there. Has been since the beginning of time. From the day that you are born until the day that you die, something wants to take what you have. To name a few: plagues, viruses, famines, droughts, hurricanes, tornadoes, wildfires, bacteria, floods, cold spells, hot spells, spoiled food, wild animals, tame animals, wild people, accidents, meteorites, sun spots, radiation, falling trees, gravity, exploding gas grills, carbon monoxide, falls off roofs, bad people, and everyday stupid stuff.

"And then your body takes over: You're worn out, lonesome, can't sleep at night, can't stay awake in the day, friends gone, money gone, folks gone, teeth fall out, ears are ringing, can't see, everything you eat makes you sick except ice cream, pain in every joint, and all you have to look forward to is pain and suffering, and you're ready for the kingdom to come – if they'll let you in. And, if not, they throw you in a fiery pit with the devil for all eternity.

"And you got the nerve to ask me: 'Am I afraid of Judgment Day and if I'm listed in the Book of Life?' You bet your life! And I got a lot to answer for!"

"I see your point," the visitor replied. A smile then creeped across his face as he relaxed his aggressive tone. "I arrived to weigh your achievements on these scales and ask you one more question: Are you ready to go? I already knew your answer but I wanted to know if you knew the answer. It's not God's will that any soul be lost but all have the chance to work out their own salvation. So, I've decided to give you a reprieve: for the present."

Eddy was shocked: "What does this all mean? Listen, I'm not planning on going anywhere right this moment and what do I need a reprieve from? I may be down but I'm not out! And, I've been wanting to ask you a question: Why do you look so much like me? – it's like looking in a mirror."

"Don't get excited, Eddy. I know this appearance of mine is disturbing but I did not want to scare you too much before I finish this mission. Looking at one's own face tends to make mankind feel more at ease than looking at a stranger. I will leave you with this message: Your future depends on one person – you! Soon, you will be charged with some tough decisions before I return with these scales. I will be back! I want to meet The Deacon. He's in there somewhere and wants to burst out. There is work to do. By the way, my name is Michael."

The visitor then pulled his gold sash down low to shadow his stern eyes as he backed toward the door. I noticed that his gait was like that of a floating shuffle and not exactly a walk. I tried but I could not yell out what I was thinking: "Man, if I wasn't scared before, I am now!"

The visitor must have read my concerns and my questions because he paused: "Your time is not yet, but instead a reprieve. But there is a mandate if you are to become the person that you were meant to be. Discover The Shield!"

"And: What man is he that liveth and shall not see death? Shall he deliver his soul from the hand of the grave?"

The door to my office shut behind my visitor. I rushed to the window to see where he was headed and what I saw was baffling: A black horse standing in my front yard. Then, the visitor mounted, and it was like poof and they were gone into the air!

Not fully understanding what had just transpired, I slid back into my chair. I mumbled: "Well, that went well. I guess he doesn't need my services. What do you suppose that he is selling me or telling me?"

The mandate. "What does that mean? Who was that guy? Why pick on me? Did I do something to the mob? Maybe he is just a crackpot full of self-righteousness and drunk to boot. That's it, he's just a nut!"

Having tempered my anxiety, I pulled the shades, turned off the light, locked the door, and made my way to the back room where I fell into bed for an anticipated restless night of wondering. "Deliver my soul from the hand of the grave. Wow, did that just happen? Was all of this just one of my bad dreams? And, how does he know about The Deacon? And how do I find that shield?"

Then a chilling thought slapped me right in the face! I jumped up and looked around: "Where's my check? It was lying right here on my desk!" There was no check and there was no sign of Michael. "Did Michael take that check? If he did, he will need more than that Arab sword!"

Chapter Six

"Mammon Is Easy to Like"

I arrived at Domino's after lunch – about 2:30. I wanted to case out the joint beforehand so I could stay those two steps ahead. Everything seemed normal, so I found a table at the back, in the dark, and secluded. I muttered to myself: "Did I want the money so bad that I would paint myself into a corner? Yeah, I guess I do."

What will Eddy Riffle do for money? How far will he go? Is his mind so cluttered with guilt that he will become a "lover of money" just to satisfy his quest for self-punishment? How much can his conscience tolerate?

Eddy's business connection with "The Employer of Bought Souls" will present him with a unique opportunity for wealth and mischief. In his mind, he feels that this course in the only choice. He needs cash for his family and for himself. He might do anything!

"For what shall it profit a man, if he shall gain the whole world, and lose his own soul?" Mark 8:36.

"And I will say to my soul, Soul, thou hast much goods laid up for many years; take thine ease, eat, drink, and be merry. But God said unto him, Thou fool, this night thy soul shall be required of thee; then whose shall those things be, which thou hast provided?" Luke 12:19-20

Next morning: For the next hour or so, I found myself struggling through coffee and donuts on my way to waking myself. I could not get those crazy thoughts out of my mind. "Was that goofball for real or was it all a nightmare?" And, my concentration was not that great this morning. It was like I was still asleep. To boot: I still had icing on my fingers and on my face and my fresh-from-the-dry-cleaners suit had a big coffee spot right on my lapel just under my chin. "Great! There are things that I must still do alright like wiping the sugar off my nose and blotting my lapel. What a joke. And, I ain't forgot about that check, Michael!"

Ring, ring, ring, ring, ring, ring, and ring: "Somebody must be having a bad day and needs me in a hurry. I hope they know the shape I'm in – not good!" I always let the phone ring seven times just to make sure they really want me. Besides, today I hoped they would hang up –"I don't need another sad story." But I answered anyway: "Hello, this is Eddy Riffle, your private detective for all needs and your attorney at law to keep it all legal."

"Well, good morning, Mr. Private-Eye and Mr. Mouth-Piece. This is Mr. Client – but some people just started calling me Bub – like you. I want to see you right away. Don't try to talk – just listen! Meet me at Domino's about three o'clock, today. Don't tell anyone and don't call your detective buddy down on the force. We know about Sam Holler! It's worth big bucks to you. We are trusting you for the time being, so don't foul this up, get me?"

"I'll be there, Bub – I could use the cash. By now you know me and how I operate. If I take a job, I'm yours. Just remember: I don't take a case if it'll send me to jail, or worse. Is that suitable? And I haven't talked to Sam – since whenever."

Reply: "This one will be a legal close call but you are a smart guy – being a savvy attorney and all. Figure it out so that you are ethical. It's that simple. Be here on time! The capo will be at the confab so be on good behavior – he's watching you closely."

I made my way over to the safe, opened it and withdrew my police-special .38-caliber, 5-shot revolver. I slid that safety backup pistol into my waistband in the back and underneath my coat. "This might be dangerous. I hope I don't need this!" Mr. Client's capo was a big-time mobster that dealt in payola and collusion, illegal money laundering, vice, gambling, prostitution, and maybe a little worse. It's funny how things that used to be against the law are not anymore – just ignored. I didn't want to know too much about The Employer because that was dangerous! This much I did know: "He bought souls – hook, line, and sinker – once in, there's no getting out – except feet first!"

I arrived at Domino's after lunch – about 2:30. I wanted to case out the joint beforehand so I could stay those two steps ahead. Everything seemed normal, so I found a table at the back, in the dark, and secluded. I muttered to myself: "Did I want the money so bad that I would paint myself into a corner? Yeah, I guess I do."

The back door to Domino's opened. Mr. Client, The Employer, and a few ugly men barged their way into the place like they were the chief cook and bottle washer. In fact, they were! And, I already knew just enough: They were well connected to the right people and not to be messed with or denied. If you knew too much, you faced a lit fuse. Hold that firecracker in your hand a bit too long and ouch! "Oh boy, what am I signing up for?"

"Hi, Eddy. Nice booth," said Mr. Client. "Let the boys check you over – you know the routine – nothing personal. After all, you are a business friend of mine and I need your services. You've helped us a little in the courts now and then, so I think that it's time we moved you up in the chain. Get where I'm going?"

Looking at the situation that I had gotten myself into, I thought it best to confess without answering. "If I'm a friend, I'd hate to see your enemies." He laughed and that eased the tension. "I have my usual protection so tell the boys not to get alarmed. Nothing personal – just my work tools." The Employer, a.k.a. the capo, sat nearby and casually sipped on a cola while playing with his phone. Bub was the emcee for this performance.

After a little laughing and joking and some rough frisking, I proved to be a man of my word. They let me keep my backup .38 and my .45 in my waistband. After all, I hadn't heard the deal yet. Mr. Client: "Eddy, what I have to tell you might get you into a lot of trouble so don't rat on us or let us down. Walk out now if it sounds too big. Do I make my point very clear?"

"Yes, crystal. Let her rip!"

"Eddy, we need a gumshoe-mouthpiece just like you. Someone that the police, especially your buddy Detective Holler, trusts – sometimes. And, that person must be above suspicion when visiting police headquarters – maybe. This is a big job and if you are not 100 percent with us, you best be leaving Domino's now! I don't want to scare you but I will. I know that you have bent the rules before or you wouldn't be a PI and that you'll do things just for the money. Right?"

"Right, but with limitations – I won't ever kill or rob anybody! This must be in the contract or I walk." The capo casually nodded his acceptance.

Mr. Client proceeded: "We are in agreement. But, we've checked and found that you were a religious man of the past – don't let that Deacon guy get in our way or else it's deep six for the both of you. We won't ask you to turn your back on your religious entertainment but keep it in check. Now, take this package with you. Included is a book about a fictitious business and how they handled their money transactions. There are no names mentioned in this book. And, after reading, you will understand what it is that we require. So, take off and remember who it is that you are dealing with."

I took the package: "I'm good, see you around." Bub showed me to the back door: "Eddy, I need you to start on this project right away, so get moving!" The Employer did not speak to me during the whole meeting – he just sized me up one side and down the other.

I left Domino's and walked back to my office, just to clear my head. What was I going to do? I wanted the money but I had my limitations of how to make it. My Biblical memory was rushing to my brain. "Blessed are the poor in spirit. Blessed are they that mourn. Blessed are the merciful. Blessed are the peacemakers. Blessed are the meek. Blessed are the persecuted. Blessed are those that seek righteousness. Blessed are the pure in heart and a whole bunch more that was blessed." I was now on a path of not being any of them that were blessed and my conscience was again becoming bothersome.

Later at the office: I opened the package and spent the next four hours reading the material. Some book! It was nothing other than marching orders for a good attorney to set up fake corporations to launder money derived from the family business. My cut was big bucks and if I took their cash, I would be on easy street and I could help send my two grandsons to college – one of these days. So, I told myself: "I'm not hurting anybody. I'm just doing some legal paperwork and that's what I'm trained for – O.K.!"

It was now past midnight and I was tired. I told myself that I would sleep on it and decide in the morning "Who am I kidding? I going to do it, and that's that!" Then, something popped into my thoughts: "Lovers of money/greedy – is that me? So, what – back off you watch-dog!"

The next week I worked diligently and I was starting to feel some relief from my mental anguish and twinges of a nagging conscience. And I had completed the paperwork for setting up dummy corporations and was ready to deliver. The illicit money would soon be rolling into my grubby hooks, trash cans full. "Oh, yeah – happy me!"

I dialed Mr. Client: "This is Eddy. We are good to go. Everything is filed with the appropriate government agencies for their review and processing. It should be no problem. When the clerk saw your name on the forms, she started calling me 'Sir.' But, if anything does come up or if some wise guy gets frisky, we might need to grease a few palms. We just need to relax for now and wait for their rubber stamp before accounts can be initiated. We're on our way to a three-point mutual relationship – I deliver, you prosper, you pay Eddy."

Mr. Client: "I knew that you were the right man for the job, Eddy. Pleasure doing business with a public servant like you. And there's another bonus waiting for you – that's point number three. Just come by our Tampa shop down at Pier 5 tonight and pick it up. I think you will like the way we do business. If you want to watch and learn, get there early."

"Thanks, I'll be there."

I just hung up the phone with Bub when things began to change: ring, ring, ring, ring, ring, ring, and ring! On the other end: "Hello, this is Holler, you know, Detective Sam Holler. How's it going, Deacon?"

Eddy acting surprised: "You mean Sam Holler – that old hound dog from FSU – still validating parking tickets? I've got a desk drawer full of those aggravating blue slips. And, nobody calls me The Deacon anymore. Whatever, it's good to hear from you."

"O.K. Eddy, I'll cut to the chase. I need to see you right away. It's official business. I'm your long-time friend so I want to give you a heads-up and a little advice. I need to do this today – for your sake!"

"Alright with me, Sam. I have an appointment and I'll stop on the way. Can't be too important if they put you in charge of this quizzing session.

Remember that I finished ahead of you at FSU. You were last in our class and I was next to last. Ha!"

"Very funny, just get here as soon as you can and to me, you're still The Deacon."

Later, down at the precinct: "Come on in Eddy and sit down. You know Detective Booth. He is here as a material witness. Before we start, you have the right to have an attorney present besides yourself – maybe you should get a smart one."

"Now Sam, that's cold, man! And, it's not very amusing coming from an old friend and college buddy. I'll waive anything you want. I got nothing to hide."

"Eddy, we have here before us a stack of applications for Certification of Incorporation that lists Mr. Client as Chief Operations Officer and you as Lead Attorney. Are you associating with that hood? We have a file on him that needs two 4-drawer cabinets to hold it all. This is not good and looks bad for you in the worst way. We are friends and I just want to help you and keep you out of big trouble."

"Well, Sam, all I'm doing is some legal work for my client and besides, I need the money. My grandsons want to go to college someday and it's my job to help them get there. You understand? I've done nothing illegal. What's a granddad supposed to do?"

"Alright, Eddy, I don't want to alarm you, if you're on the level. It's just that we've received a few suspicious tips about Mr. Client's underworld connections and about these new so-called business endeavors that involve you. We know all about their money laundering rackets. Hard cash taken from illegal means is delivered to your Mr. Client and he takes it from there. He distributes the cash to and from these dummy corporations that have offshore accounts. Great setup and he gets big bucks from the action."

Detective Boone then edged closer to Eddy. He entered the conversation: "Mr. Riffle, may I interject with some advice? One should be careful not to take for granted another's charity. If you are somewhat on a leash, don't infringe on their patience because choke holds are not pleasant – just ask my dog." He then gave a short wink in Eddy's direction.

Eddy looked puzzled and responded: "Well, I'm sure that advice will be taken to heart if I can figure out what it means."

Sam had heard enough babble from Detective Boone and ended the chitchat: "Take off, you rascal, and remember to watch yourself and what you are willing to do for your clients. I'd hate to have to arrest my buddy – who would I beat at golf?"

I left Precinct 777 with apprehension because Sam knew more about Mr. Client's operations than I did and that could lead to disaster. But still on my mind: "Tonight, my next stop will be Pier 5 to get my bonus. Money always makes me feel better!"

Later: Pier 5, Tampa, was way down at the end of the docks where it was the darkest. There was one single little light above the large hangar doors. The sign above read A. Baddon Enterprises. I mused to myself: "This is one of those new corporations I legalized. I can almost see my cut neatly stacked before me in easy to spend small bills."

Not wanting to make my presence known just yet, I slid around to the backside, climbed up a convenient drainpipe, and sneaked through the roof door. I was able to find a nice viewing spot just above the main working area of the hangar. I wanted to see what kind of outfit I had hooked up with and how much trouble I was in.

It didn't take long before those big doors rolled up to a screeching halt. Two white limos pulled inside. Neatly dressed men piled out of those limos. They had automatic machine guns that they pointed in all directions. Thank heavens they didn't look up in my direction. I hunkered down and held my breath. If they saw me, they would blast me right off my perch. My mind blurted a thought: "If The Deacon is present, he needs to say a little prayer for me!"

The door to the office opened and out walked Mr. Client, The Employer, and a dozen familiar men that also had automatic machine guns. Each one of those men looked just as mean as the one beside him. One twitch and the whole place would go up in a hail of gunfire. "What am I doing here?"

After much conversation and passing of good tidings, they got down to business. A fellow that The Employer called Mr. Sharda did the negotiating and the hand shaking. Then, the trunks of those white limos were opened and exposed the contents to my wide eyes – cash. That's right, cash, the trunks were full of cash!

The meeting was concluded and the participants got into their vehicles and exited leaving Mr. Client literally swimming in cash. He jumped right into that big pile of currency and started swimming. His men laughed and laughed. Bottles were opened and drinking started. It was a very successful day. In all this delight and confusion, I caught a glimpse of a man in the background and over by the office. He looked to me like a dead-ringer for Detective Boone. He tried to be inconspicuous by using a pile of tires as his lurking spot and a good barrier if gunshots had been required.

I had seen all that I needed to see and slipped from my hiding spot, back out onto the roof, down the drainpipe, and then around to the front. The doors had now been closed shut so I knocked on the side door. I heard clicking like the sound of bullets being chambered in those automatic machine guns. I heard the rustling of feet as they rushed to the other side of the door. Then a voice: "Who's there?" I let out a big: "It's Eddy Riffle, let me in, I'm here to see Bub – I mean Mr. Client!"

The door opened and there they stood – all pointing weapons right at my forehead. I could only think of one thing to say: "Is this a private party or can anyone join in?"

Mr. Client then looked at his men and then they looked back at him. They all broke out in loud laughter. They pulled me inside, slapped me on the back, gave me a swig out of a bottle, and handed me a Cuban cigar. I lit the thing, took another swig, and joined the party that lasted and lasted and lasted. "I will have a headache tomorrow!"

The Sting Operation

The next morning at my office, I did have that headache and I felt awful. I wasn't sure which was worse – my headache or my fret over Mr. Client and his financial business operations. I opened my desk lap drawer and the first thing I saw was a check for my cut of that money shuffling business. "Wow! Just another big check – $25,000." I realized that it was a very good payday for a little dishonesty, but I did wrestle with myself about being a bought soul. So, after a good slugfest with my conscience, I concluded that I could not and would not be part of this crime ring. My heart and soul knew it was wrong and I felt emotionally compelled to do something – "he's not going to own me!" So, I called my law enforcement buddy: "Sam, this is Eddy. I have to confess that I have not been a good boy. And, I'm afraid that I have some startling news that you need to hear."

I explained all about the capo, Mr. A. Baddon's (a.k.a. – The Employer of Bought Souls) and the illegal operations and Mr. Client's involvement. Also, I told him about Detective Boone and what I saw at the pier. He was naturally upset about his companion's connection. He immediately contacted the District Attorney and set up a secret meeting. A plan was subsequently devised and I was included in the action. And, I had to turn over that check for 25k to the District Attorney and that put me in the DA's good graces – for the first time!

Sam said that he did not want me to be in any more danger than necessary, so he limited my involvement. All I had to do was to determine when Mr. Client was to receive another shipment of cash from Mr. Sharda, the date, and the time. "So much for limited involvement." I knew that I had to be precise so as not to be detected because I was dealing with certain death if I failed. It was a gamble but I had to take the chance. I was betting on the jackpot with my last centavo.

At the usual monthly business meeting where the capo sits at the head of the table: "To my worker bees, I have to say that it's been a good month, financially speaking. All of you will be happy with your paychecks." He then took out a pile of envelopes and passed them out. To my surprise, who do you think was sitting at the big-boy table beside Mr. Client and got a fat check? That's right – Mr. Macks – another sold out soul – without much choice – and I had a hand in it!

The Employer continues: "Further, we can thank Eddy Riffle, who's sitting at the rear, for setting up the legal stuff so we can do our unique business like we want. Thanks, Eddy! You get a lot of attention but I don't want the rest of the team to be jealous." The boys all politely snickered. This jovial atmosphere allowed for some sniping among the attendees and that's when Mr. Macks and I caught sight of each other. Just for old time sake, we nodded and tipped our hats. I grinned because his nose was scarred from my double-jab and right cross.

Mr. Client then stood up and excused me from the meeting: "No use you knowing the operational plans, Eddy, it will just get you into trouble if anything goes wrong. The less you know the better for you."

What they didn't know: while sitting at the rear, I was able to place a "bug" under the table that would pick up his entire plan. And, Sam was located outside the building in an unmarked police van that was recording all the conversations down to the last detail. Discussed were names, dates, and places – delivered as ordered – now go and hide!

The rest is police history. I located myself in my usual hiding spot before Pier 5 was raided. I witnessed a long and harsh gun battle. As it turned out, The Employer was the only man that was killed in the gunfire. There was a lot of noise but poor marksmanship – holes in everything but the targets. While totally pinned down, The Employer simply charged the machine guns of the police – a suicide attack – 100% sure. He asked for it and he got it – looked like he wanted to make a point! Maybe it was because he failed to buy another prized soul, me. And, with his devil's temper, he must have been temporarily filled with remorse for being tricked. I personally was relieved that he was gone for good and not able to seek revenge for my tattle-tale.

A well-hidden Detective Boone and Mr. Client were both arrested sneaking out the side window and pleaded that they were coming in and not going out. Mr. Sharda was arrested. He said that he was there to get his car repaired. There were 58 bullet holes in it. The rest of the wounded members of the gang were arrested – they were there for bingo. The confiscated cash from the sting was big bucks which subsequently got deposited into the police anti-crime fund – minus enough for 3 dozen donuts. The success of the sting was kept secret and my name was never mentioned to the press or to anybody. Judge Rule was informed of my involvement. She commented: "I knew he was made of good stuff!"

That bonus check for $25,000 from the mob was kept by the city for evidence and then donated to the police widows' charity. Detective Sam Holler was promoted to Lieutenant of Investigations. He thanked me privately. We are still buddies.

But there was a hitch: An autopsy revealed something odd. The cold dead body of Mr. A. Baddon (no nick-names on a toe tag) contained one standard police bullet and one stray rifle round – the one that inflicted the kill shot. It checked out to be the same caliper of a sniper rifle.. A puzzled Sam felt that it was his duty to ask Eddy a few questions.

"According to your military records, you fired expert with the M-14, M-16, .45-cal. pistol, and the M-79 grenade launcher. Is that right, Eddy?"

"Yes, but what are you driving at – am I a suspect of something?"

"No, nothing like that, yet. Everything turned out for the best, it had to be done. It doesn't matter who did the kill shot or why – it's bad man down! But did you see anybody moving up high? If it was a sniper, then it could be a murder case. And, there's something else: The body of The Employer disappeared from the morgue, no trace."

"What's this have to do with me?"

"Do you own a rifle – a bolt-action 7.62x51mm M24 with accuracy to 800 meters? I'm being exact for a reason. It's a standard-issue sniper rifle for the military."

"Yes, but it's in storage in my attic. I haven't got it down or cleaned it for 40 years. Check it if you like!"

"Anything else that you recall that might assist the investigation?"

"Might have been some shadows darting but that's about all."

"Alright, Eddy, that's it for now. I'll look at that rifle tomorrow, so don't touch it for any reason. And don't forget to show up for your award presentation."

A few days later, the mayor held a closed-door ceremony and gave Eddy a medal. After shaking everybody's hand multiple times, he made his way out of the event feeling great and unable to hide that big smile that was all over his grubby face. He was elated because he had done something right for a change. "After all, it's a step in the right direction and Mr. A. Baddon, The Employer of Bought Souls, is out of business – permanent. But who shot him – a sniper?"

Eddy began to worry: "Am I having real dreams or dreaming real. Something is happening to me and my psyche. Am I losing my mind?"

Eddy needed to stay in good graces, so while appearing in the public view, Eddy raised verbal havoc with the brutal police and their outrageous tactics. And, to show loyalty to the family, he spared no quarter when defending Mr. Client before the courts.

A mutual deal: Mr. Client pled guilty to a misdemeanor in attempting to commit a crime but arrived too late for the party – caught entering a side window. He thereby received a time-served sentence. He was released.

Because of years of public service and to get him lost in the shuffle, Detective Boone was allowed to retire to the beaches of Florida to walk his dog and to live out the rest of his life. Judge G. R. Rule presided at the trials and to avoid suspicion, reflected remorse at the light sentences that she was legally required to render.

Several months later, Detective Boone was found lying in ocean waters just off the beach and near his residence. Cause of death: drowning with possible implications.

Sam Holler began to worry: "Is Eddy Riffle fading back into Vietnam and has turned his dreams into acts of violence? I could be wrong but I'll watch him very close. I hope it's just my imagination. But he does have the same type of rifle used in the killing of The Employer. But when I checked it, I could not verify that it had been recently discharged. It had been totally cleaned and cleaned."

The Association

Eddy Riffle, Lt. Sam Holler, and Judge G. R. Rule entered into a secret association. Mr. Riffle would remain under the confidence of Mr. Client's crime family and continue to act as their mouthpiece and legal expert. Assignment: Gather information of criminal activity and act accordingly to

bring such culprits to justice. Eddy will get the evidence and show they lied –
Sam will get them tried – the judge will get them jailed.

Lt. Holler was beginning to suspect that all was not copacetic with Eddy's
mental state – like schizophrenia. So, he decided to watch Eddy closely and
maybe he could help or maybe he would have to make an arrest or maybe put
him into a straitjacket. "I can't let him knock off criminals indiscriminately
before I get them to trial!"

Judge Rule was kept informed about the situation, but she wanted to
make sure before taking action; one way or the other. Afterall, he was
her Public Defender and in a position of trust. Any punishment would
be harsh, by necessity.

Chapter Seven

The Alligator Clown

In this chapter, Abaddon changes his appearance to that of "The Alligator Clown" (so Eddy would not recognize him as Mr. A. Baddon, The Employer). His purpose was a unique and devious plan of revenge! He was out played once by Eddy Riffle when The Employer of Bought Souls was stopped cold by a sniper's bullet. He believes that Eddy did the job. And, it hurt his devilish feelings. Fallen angels are not empowered to kill anyone, but they can make one's life miserable with temptations and illusions.

"Woe to the inhabitants of the earth and of the sea! for the devil is come down unto you, having great wrath, because he knoweth that he hath but a short time." Rev. 12:12

"Submit yourselves therefore to God. Resist the devil, and he will flee from you." James 4:7

A knock on my office door. Sliding under was an envelope. I opened the door. No one there! That was unusual – no la-tee-das – just that sealed document. Cautiously, I peeled the flap and found a note: "Referred to you by a mutual business acquaintance, Mr. Client." I wanted to throw that red flag in the can, but with him involved, it could be rewarding!

I paused for a thought: "It's a good thing that this person doesn't know that I put our mutual acquaintance in jail; albeit, a short stint."

After the commute of Mr. Client's prison sentence that he incurred in that Pier 5 bust, I was promoted to top-dog in the handling of the family's legal matters. Bub trusts me and he doesn't suspect anything, but one slip and my gigs up and my goose is cooked!

Continuing with the note: "My life is in danger and I need immediate protection to avoid a hit-man's bullet. If interested, meet me on College Street today at 1:00 P.M. – at the Moonpie & RCCola Café. Pick an outside table and be in open view of the Gator football parade. I will be in disguise and dressed in an alligator clown suit – I can't trust anybody."

"An alligator clown suit – should be simple to spot, right? The one with the big jaws!"

Being that this was the Homecoming parade for the rivalry game, a few dozen clowns would be rambling about the streets and dressed in all sorts of weird mascot outfits. With all the commotion of the celebration, there would be no way to pick out "my" clown. But I did as I was instructed and headed for the café. When I arrived, I found the place amuck with fools. The raucous crowd waved gator signs and some had bulldog signs. Both sides wanted to swat the other side. But, most of them were young and would outlive any sowing-of-oats.

I glanced back and forth at each passing alligator head trying to find a clue because I don't like surprises. One thing I had to remember: "Keep up the guise – I'm supposed to be low-down and self-serving, so act the part."

The parade was proceeding as expected when the Gainesville College marching band high-stepped their way down the crowded street. Loud music coupled with the clatter of the audience yelling: "stomp-the-dogs," quieted my apprehension about the task at hand.

I stood up briefly and then sat back down only to be startled by an alligator clown sitting beside me. It was a great disguise because there was no way I could identify this person because all alligators look alike, but the body size and shape indicated that it probably was a female. I whispered to my new guest: "You stop by for a quick beer or a moon pie?"

The response: "Quiet, I think that I'm being followed!"

The clown person seemed to be in a rush and quickly reached into a backpack and pulled out a zipped money bag and slapped it down on the table with a thud. A bit surprised, I cautiously picked it up and peeked inside. It was a large amount of cash; looked like many thousands. "Bingo-payday!"

A thought entered my mind. "This could be big, too big for me! My survival instinct took over. I looked about for any sign of danger or if there was any place for cover so I could dive under and yell for Mama! But no one around us seemed to be caring much about a fully dressed parade alligator clown talking with another simple clown that was dressed in a wrinkled raincoat, a floppy detective hat and a half-loose tie. It was hard to tell which costume was the scariest; hers or mine?"

It eased my tensions when I witnessed nothing suspicious; like a killer hanging out of a three-story apartment window and aiming an M-24 high-precision long range rifle at my clown's head. So, I spoke up calmly and in my best authority: "Let me have the whole story. No time for short cuts or croc talk. It's time to get serious!"

"Mr. Riffle, I'm in deep trouble and don't know where to turn. My business partner wants to have me shot dead before I spoil his ambitious plans. He and I are partners in a project that is of the highest importance. Our Aeronautical Engineering Systems company recently invented an artificial intelligence breakthrough; one that is able to efficiently hijack rogue intercontinental ballistic missiles and safely reroute them back to source for detonation and/or neutralize the threat. Such a discovery will revolutionize the determent of many weapons of mass-destruction; it could change the order of world power!"

"So, what's the problem? Sounds great to me and should be a money maker. Uncle Sam will pay plenty for the rights because the good old USA has to make sure that it stays the world-leader in all categories. So, where do I come in – a lowly PI?"

The Clown: "Well there's a fly in the ice cream as to who will get control of this new technology? My partner, Mr. Charlatan Jones, has been contacted by a foreign terroristic entity and they offered him riches beyond belief and it's all tax free; about fifty million dollars. He accepted their offer while having little thought for the USA. He's a dirty traitor!"

The Clown, continuing: "Just the other day when CJ was in the process of copying our secret codes and systems, I caught him red-handed. I reacted and vehemently objected and threatened to call the authorities. With egg on his deceitful face still drying, he recanted and told me that he would do the right thing and contact the FBI. But as it turned out, this was just a ploy to give him time to eliminate obstacles such as his very own partner! By accident, I subsequently intercepted his emails and found out that he had hired a killer by the name of Zyler. I immediately called my confidant at The Daily Bugle and found out that this Zyler is an evil mouth-closer, a sniper. And, he has a reputation of having no trace of a conscience."

Eddy thought it best to milk the situation: "I repeat – what can I do? I'm just an ordinary private investigator without much backbone for suicide missions. This whole thing is way over my head. We both will be killed if this is not handled correctly. I have a wife, two daughters, and two grandkids that I want to send to college. But, wait a second, how much did you say would be my cut in this fiasco – in rounded big numbers?"

The Clown answered: "The cash in that envelop that you are holding is yours just for listening, so how about an additional 100 grand? But one condition: I must stay alive to pay, so you have to ensure my safety. CJ is a fast worker and it's all going down tomorrow night. We have to be ready. No time to waste!"

Eddy reacted: "You said the secret word – 100 Gs. I'm in with both feet! Cashier's check and I must see it before I will even think about saving you or the world!"

Sarcastic clown: "Oh, alright, I will have it with me tomorrow, but you only get to look. My office is on the first floor. I'll meet you there."

The clown then gave me a detailed layout of the office building along with her plan for me to surprise CJ in the act of treason, to wit: a midnight exchange meeting with a terrorist agent. CJ's fifty-million-dollar payday was on its way and that was his main concern.

"It's wise for a private investigator to never trust anyone's plan but his own – to do so has led many to sudden impact – like being knocked off one's perch into a tank of ice-cold water at a carnival baseball throw – breathtaking but with a wake-up call!"

Before departing the scene, The Clown revealed that she was scared that Zyler would be lurking at this meeting and would take her out, permanently; the classic double-cross. CJ has lied to her about everything and is setting her up for the mouth-closure. He made sure that she would be at the meeting. In death she could not talk and if the deal was discovered, she would be blamed for every dirty deed that CJ had perpetrated.

Sounded like a feasible plan, but for Eddy, realization suddenly arrived by slow coach. "This is happening too fast. Also, I have not seen The Clown's face except through alligator teeth and I've got a hunch; she is hiding something. I was hired to protect her life but now I face a dangerous network of spies, lies, and greed. And, I have not established anyone's true identity. If wrong, I will go to jail, or worse! Also, what about Zyler? He could be there to mop the floors. What if it turns out that he is just the janitor and merely has soapsuds in his mop bucket? And, what if his only mouth-closing knowledge is from biting down on his dentures?"

Eddy does his best thinking or sleeping while leaning back in that lousy rocking chair that he cherishes. So, that's where he headed – to his comfort zone. With feet propped up, a little of the red wine for the stomach sake, and as soft music played, he buzzed himself into slumber.

Later, with stiff neck, he awoke to a figure standing in the dark shadows. What now? The smokey image spoke: "Think Eddy, think and beware of The Clown – deception with lips of trickery – such things are prophesied – arrival of false prophets and wolves in sheep's clothing or alligator heads – protect yourself!" The image then faded back into the darkness from whence it had appeared.

"I know what I have to do. I'll call Sam Holler and activate The Association to operational mode – this will be our first real mission – foul it up and it will be my last!"

Plan A was developed; good luck! There is no B-Plan. With that thought, Eddy provided himself with his own backup plan. As usual, his hide was first priority!

Next day, the action commenced – 11:30 P.M… As planned, Eddy made his way into the building through an unlocked entry door. He made his way to The Clown's office – just to verify that she was where she was supposed to be and that she actually possessed his certified check for $100,000. She was seated with her back to a glass window. Eddy could not see her face, but he could see his check in her hand as she waved it back and forth. She did not turn to greet Eddy. The alligator head was lying on the desk beside her.

Up the back stairs he bolted to the 12th floor and into an unlocked room next to CJ's office. Eddy had full view through a mirror. He could see CJ and his entire office area. CJ could not see Eddy. It was a one-way, two-sided mirror. He flipped on the video recorder – action, camera.

The clock struck midnight. It was time for Eddy to act and get the ball rolling. He burst through the doorway and shouted at CJ: "Reach for the sky you smirking traitor! Don't make a move and I won't shoot your bow-tie off. If you have done nothing wrong then sit still and finish smoking that cigar. I won't hurt you!"

CJ, shocked by this sudden attack, choked on cigar smoke – that which was supposed to be exhaled was instead swallowed. His eyes rolled back into his head and he passed out cold and slumped over his desk. Eddy turned off the lights to surprise the next invitee.

Time twelve o' clock midnight… The hallway door squeaked opened. A muscular man clothed in a business suit entered the darkened room. He was carrying a briefcase handcuffed to his left wrist. His right hand was filled with a hot cup of coffee. Eddy reacted quickly. He turned on the lights. "Who might you be?" The man did not answer and did not try to physically respond. Eddy surmised that the shoulder bulge within the man's suit coat was a holstered pistol. So, they just stared at each other, but not for long.

Not according to plan: An adjacent secret closet door then flapped open. It was The Clown with her face painted red and in an all-black costume and she was pointing an M-16 rifle! "Drop them weapons, boys!"

Eddy dropped his 45 and raised his hands. CJ, just waking from his shock, dropped off again. The supposed terrorist agent slowly dropped his shoulder pistol. His face indicated that he was just as surprised as Eddy.

The Clown spoke in a high-ringing voice that startled Eddy. "Do exactly as I say and you three dumbos can live a little longer! As for you, Mister agent-man, unlock those handcuffs or die on the spot!" He obliged and handed over the briefcase.!

A few moments passed as she quickly investigated the contents; ten million dollars in cash and forty million dollars in demand bonds payable, same as cash, at a bank located somewhere in Transylvania – no questions asked.

"I don't require your silly money but with this cash, I will buy all the misconduct that I can muster. Money talks to you weak-spirited human creations. Temptation is your weakness and you will do anything for money."

She closed the briefcase and smiled a weird lip-twist. Wow, she was ugly – looked like the devil and just as mean. Growling: "As always, I finish deceitful ploys by leaving no innocent witnesses to beg their God for mercy. And, it's my pleasure to let all of you know one little tiny-tiny thing. I'm not a nice angel and I don't like nice people or nice angels. As a matter of fact, I don't like any people. To prove it, I'm going to destroy your fantastic new life-saving technology just so somebody will eventually blow this whole planet of earth to smithereens – bit by bit. And, take every human being along for the grand finale! Satan's treat!"

Wasting no time, she ordered the three intended victims to line up against the wall. "Hands behind heads! I like to be sloppy when someone is to be properly obliterated." CJ who could not stand, was helped to his feet by Eddy. All he wanted to know was what was happening; he had no idea.

Eddy's was getting scared: "Where is the help?" Eddy forced himself to think. He needed to delay that evil force. So, he took a chance and yelled out: "It's crunch time. Hear me, Sam. It's crunch time, Sam!"

The Clown looked concerned. "Who's Sam? Did you call upon the mighty Samuel? How do you know Samuel who came forth and was established to be a mighty prophet and then anointed David to be King of Israel? So, who are you to call out for this powerful man?"

Eddy realized that he must keep the clown distracted so Sam Holler would have time to do his job and smash down the door. "Yea, me and Samuel are close and he would be awful mad if you did something to his buddy. You know that he is not to be poked, so what is it that you want of us?"

In a loud shrieking voice: "This is that spirit of antichrist, whereof ye have heard that it should come; and even now already it is in the world."

Still shrieking: "Samuel cannot help you. I've got all of you in my clutches. You think that this Samuel will deliver your sorry souls from my destruction. It won't work. You desire this powerful "anti-weapon of mass destruction" to save lives but I do not. I want blood! You are a pest and must be exterminated. Bring on Samuel and I will blast him too!"

With Samuel not present, the wicked minion raised her M-16 rifle, took aim and placed her finger on the trigger and began to squeeze. She blared: "Good-bye boys – see you on the other side – do you like it hot – some do? If Samuel is close by and hiding then he needs to make it quick – say, in the next second! The first bullet is for you, tattle-tale, Eddy Riffle. I dug it out of my own flesh and now return it with the vengeance of Mr. Employer – remember him? I'll enjoy your punishment more than the money – you wily human."

A shocked Eddy proved her right – he was a sly fox. He did not wait for the next second or the first bullet, but attacked. He reached behind his neck for hidden ninja knives; the backup plan. His unleash of those stickers was not deadly but accurate. A ricocheted knife struck the trigger finger of the clown causing her to drop the M-16. The look on her face was disbelief like: "is my lipstick smeared?"

Plan A suddenly arrived. The door to the office was blasted to pieces. Swarming through was the city SWAT team dressed in blue menacing uniforms. Lt. Sam Holler, who led the assault exclaimed: "Someone here call for Samuel? Here I am!"

The look on the clown's face told the tale; she had been tricked. "Take me in boys – I'm yours – I'm not allowed to interfere with your human bodies – I was just teasing – Can't you take a joke? There will be another time when my hands are not tied – it's coming soon. As for you, Mr. Deacon, I'm not finished with you, yet! When the time is right, I'll be back. And then you will love what I have to offer. You will not be able to resist me. Sam Holler will not be there. If he is, I might entice him too!"

An astonished Eddy: "What do you want with me, in particular; I'm a nobody? Why am I being hounded by the devil's fallen angel troops? Is that who you are?"

"All souls are my mission. As for troops, there's a lot more of my type ready to go and some are here on earth already; gathering strength!"

Samuel, I mean Sam had heard enough of this nonsense. The clown was drug away by the neck down twelve flights of stairs. On the path across the parking lot and to the patty wagon, a rifle shot rang out! A single slug slammed into the shirt of the clown causing everyone to jump aside for cover. Sam instinctively looked up in the direction from whence the sound originated and located a single person jumping from one building to another, then gone. By the trajectory of the shot, it was later determined that it came from a 12th floor window. Lt. Sam Holler's investigative nature put two and two together. The sum: "Riffle did the shot. He was the last one to leave that 12th floor. And, he knows how to shoot and he owns the ordinance."

The assassination bullet definitely hit the target perfectly on the third button on the clown's outfit. It revealed a violent rip. But the clown did not go down and even laughed at the feeble attempt. To display her lack of fear, she opened her frilly shirt to expose a bullet wound that apparently deflected and caused no injury.

"That hiding coward of yours will fail, she shrieked. I was hit, but it glanced off my ninth rib; it's the strongest rib of them all. Eddy Riffle will pay the price for this attack – and soon!"

Authorities did try to remove the clown's costume, but it would not budge. The confiscated alligator head shriveled up into a paper ball and caught fire. Hours before her preliminary judicial hearing, The Alligator Clown mysteriously disappeared from her cell. The cell camera revealed nothing but haze and was inconclusive. Written on the wall for all to see, were these words: "The Serpent!"

Facts: Charlatan Jones (CJ) is the legit CEO of the Company. He always works until midnight. He never met The Clown nor contacted a buyer. The technology was in the development stage and awaiting approval from NASA. The mystery man with the briefcase full of counterfeit cash was a CIA operative. The plan to capture this traitorous evil doer was legally arranged by Judge Rule. "The Association" successfully rebuffed the vengeful Abaddon, A.K.A. The Alligator Clown.

"The True Soul Begins to Emerge"

Thanksgiving Day was close at hand and I was brooding. Florida's balmy breezes usually soothe my emotions and gives me feelings of optimism and hope. So, I decided to take an evening stroll down the beach and enjoy the sunset. I found a nice spot and parked myself. It was a perfect view. "Beautiful."

The solidarity was too good to last. Soon I had company. Most folks usually kept their distance for this type of entertainment, but tonight it was eerie. I noticed that up and down the beach there were many vacant sections, but next to me it was bunched with an assortment of sightseers. The common bond: "They all seemed to be hand in hand with a loved-one."

I thought it odd that they were so close when there was plenty of room, but I did enjoy their happiness and their joy of watching the sun set, together.

Then, a lady sat down beside me. "A bit crowded tonight."

"Why yes, it is. I was just about ready to call it a day."

"Me too, but it's so pretty; the sun is sitting right on the water's edge. Seems like you could just step off the ocean and into the sun; so lifelike. Don't you think?"

"Yea, my wife and I used to come here all the time and bring our daughters, but not anymore. Life changes. Nothing stays the same. Some things are good and some are not so good."

"Sorry to hear that. Hope it's fixable. Love is too precious to lose. Pride stands in the way, sometimes. We just can't seem to master that little devil."

As the sunlight began to slowly disappear, my thoughts drifted to Ellie and how our marriage was just like this picture – fading, fading, until darkness overcomes. I mumbled softly: "Must the sun always set without choice? Must love be lost without choice?"

My new acquaintance noticed my tear-filled eyes. "You know that the moon rules the night while the sun rules the day and without choice; it's God's plan of creation. The moon is a lover's light and it takes two strolling under its glow to realize that the man in the moon is like cupid; the mythical boy God of Love. Once penetrated by cupid's arrow of true love, two hearts shall become as one. Separation of this bonding back into their parts is not possible, but may seem to be so. Each half will struggle and fight within their selves until the inevitable surfaces. The cupid's arrow is strong. It can only bend, but will not break. She is waiting and hurting as much as you. Understand?"

"I sure do! Her name is Ellie!"

I jumped to my feet as I felt a sharp sting to my chest. The pain left as fast as it came. So, I composed myself as if nothing happened. I then bid farewell to this mysterious lady. We never bothered to exchange names, but I did wonder why we met so suddenly. I know that cupid is just a myth for lovers or did I just receive an arrow to the heart? I didn't see any babies flying about. Maybe that lady was cupid's mother. Anything is possible.

All that filled my mind at the moment: "I've got a baseball game to attend. Tomorrow night my grandsons will be looking for me." I rarely went to their games due to that pride thing, but this time I won't be late!

Chapter Eight

Thanksgiving Eve – Baseball – The Bully

The pitch – the swing – crack – the ball bounds toward third base – fielded by Jamie Riffle Howard – throws to first base – caught by his cousin, Aaron Riffle Howard – runner out – end of game. The kids middle name of Riffle is to honor their grandfather.

"Great play!" The scream came from behind the third base fence. It came from Grandpa Eddy Riffle. The boys heard his shout even on the bottom of a pile of exuberant teammates. They freed themselves and immediately rushed toward the grinning Eddy.

The Thanksgiving Eve baseball tournament had been fun for all until the coach from the opposing team raced onto the field and into the face of the umpire yelling: "That runner was safe by a mile – who's paying you? Are you blind, you dope?"

This particular coach had a reputation of being loud, rude, boisterous, and just a downright big-time bully. His three sons played on his team and overlooked their embarrassment because they got to play over better team members just because he was "the coach." Many complaints had been filed with the City of Orlando's Administrator of Athletics but this coach was somehow still active and just as obnoxious. Umpires for the league were unpaid volunteers and often gave in to his demands rather that argue the point. He was not liked, but tolerated!

The tirade of this coach did not stop and his speech got louder as he made his way toward the winning team's celebration – it was time for after game treats. Ellie just happened to be the coach of the winning team; Lynn and Niki were her assistants. He yelled at Ellie: "You can't seriously take this as a win. That sniveling wimp of an umpire said that it was up to you to get the call reversed. So, you better get over there and tell her that she blew the call!" Eddy and the boys, by this time, had made their way into the celebration and was busy hugging and giving high-fives. But their glee was interrupted by this tornado of rudeness heading for some face-time.

Eddy stepped forward to confront the bluster: "Settle down, man – this is my wife you're yelling at and spitting on! You don't want this to go any further and get out of hand, do you?"

"What if I do? You going to stop me, old man?"

Eddy was well trained in the dismantling of bigmouth bullies but he chose to simply give the coach "the look" because words would not be needed for this guy – just the look!

Bullies like to inflict pain on the weaker and skip out when the tide turns. If there is the slightest doubt that their victim will retaliate with some of their own hurt and misery, they generally back off especially if they get "the look." What pleasure is there to see your victim being loaded into the back of an ambulance and on the way to the hospital if you also are loaded into the same van and lying flat as a flitter? Sometimes it is hard to tell who won the boxing match – hurt is hurt!

The look: Steely-slit-fixed eyes that show no fear and a willingness to go the distance. Eddy was very experienced and could easily handle the coach but did not want a scene in front of all those families that were watching the disturbance. And, the grandsons had never seen him as anything but jovial and fun.

The bully responded: "I'll see you again when you are not hiding behind all these kids and then, Grandpappy, it won't be pleasant." He turned and walked away.

Jamie grinned at his grandpa: "Good job, gramps. That's the first time we ever saw that coach back away without getting what he wanted." Lynn and Niki hugged Eddy and said they were glad that he was there, as their fright turned to smiles.

Ellie liked it too: "Someday that brute will get what he's asking for, but hopefully not on the playing field. Violence is never the answer and not a good example for anyone."

Eddy to the team: "Your coach, Mrs. Riffle and your two great assistants are right, and besides it was my smile that got him moving away or it could have been my crooked nose – that's a sign I've been hit there a few times and one more wouldn't hurt much." The whole team laughed and some of them feinted punches to the nose. Then, off to the ice cream store – Eddy's treat.

"Have a Happy Thanksgiving with your families," was Eddy's last words to the team as he left for his office and the usual loneliness. It's tough to be alone especially during holidays. On the way home, Eddy noticed a local bar and stopped for a burger and a beer. Guess who was barely standing at the bar drinking profusely and blabbering – you guessed it! Their eyes met. The bully yelled: "Well, it's the hero of the day – come to get your Thanksgiving whipping. How about if I straightened that nose?"

Eddy did not respond but slowly began removing his belt. The bully awkwardly lunged with intent to do bodily harm. Eddy jumped aside and swiftly looped his belt over the head and around the sprawling neck of the attacker. He tightened it just enough to cut off the airflow. The surprised blowhard found himself immobile as he struggled to breathe.

Eddy had no intention of doing harm but just wanted to teach the coach a lesson. But Eddy's emotional situation never allowed for the simple. His hands began to twitch and he once again lapsed into the past – he was back in the jungles. All around him, the NVA was searching for the few remaining U.S. soldiers that was left over from an ambush. Eddy believed that he was one of the survivors and hidden in the jungle growth. An enemy soldier had approached. So, he silenced him by leaping from his hiding spot in the bush and looping his belt around the soldier's neck. He then squeezed really, really hard – he thought that his life depended on it! He was close to committing a deadly act when:

Customers, owners, bouncers, all jumped Eddy and pulled him off the coach. "You don't want to kill him, do you?"

Looking dazed and confused: "No, no, not that – anything but that. I just lost my head for a second. I'm alright now. I'm so sorry. Is he alright?"

The bully soon revived and yelled out his need for another beer. Eddy helped the coach to his feet. "Sorry, man – I lost it for a moment. You O.K.? Say, what's your name?"

Struggling, the man responded: "My name is Paul – what's yours?"

"My name is Eddy and my two grandsons play on the team that won today and my wife and daughters are the coaches. I'm sorry we got off on the wrong foot."

"You're not as sorry as I am," said Paul. "I guess I made a fool of myself today – like right now I am a certified buffoon. Not like it's the first time. It's getting to be a habit."

Eddy and Paul straightened themselves, found a table, and sipped on their beer. They shared stories and found out that they were not that far apart in life's twist and turns. Before they left the bar, they had become new friends – the kind that you can talk to without being judged and just provide a shoulder to lean on. Funny how that works – a bully can be tamed if just one friend tries.

Due to the difference in their ages, Paul felt a fatherly connection with Eddy and listened to his advice. Eddy welcomed his new friend as just that – a friend. So, they agreed to do a little fishing now and then. "Don't think that they ever made it."

Later that evening:

Ellie sits in front of a mirror and brushes her hair. Her thoughts are pleasant. She visualizes the fun of the day with the boys and the game. Her emotions are tested as she includes Eddy, her once great and only love. Remembering a love letter from long ago from her "at-war" soldier man, she opens the bottom drawer of her dresser. It was there that she protects a precious treasure of the heart. She held it to her chest with both hands. "Should I or can I, dare to remember?"

She lays the letter aside and resumes the brushing. "If I read this, I must be ready to accept the consequence. Will it open the hurt or soothe the pain I feel?"

A tear falls from a lash as she unfolds the letter that was still stained by the rainwater from a monsoon.

To my love, Ellie.

It sure is raining here. We have been hunkered down for days under our shelter halves. Not much going on and I am doing good. So, don't worry. I even had time to write you a little love note. Don't know where the words came from, but I mean every word. Here goes.

"When I was a young man and did not know you, I searched for you in many places. I did not know you at the time, but it was you that was pushing me to keep looking. When our eyes first met, the wonder of you touched me; the real me. I felt a mutual connection and a feeling that we had found ourselves, again; like we had been together in another existence. One lifetime is not long enough for the love we have to share, but that's why there is an eternity; there's a plan for us. If you are not there every day of forever then I would be heartbroken forever. As long as I keep you in the safety of my heart, you will always be with me. You are the ointment for my soul."

Well, that's about all I can write for today. The wind is picking up and hard to write out here in the boondocks. Can't wait to see you in Hawaii. Only a short time away.

I love you, my darling!

Eddy

Ellie folded the letter and placed it back in its place of safety. She has a lot to think about.

"At Home on Thanksgiving Day"

Today is Thanksgiving and another holiday without my family and a friend or two sitting around a big table stacked with food. And just the aroma of fresh-from-the-oven turkey and all the fixings always tempted to the limit and drove my gang to dig in and overeat at free will. "It's my own fault, so just wipe away all these tears and get started heating this turkey thing to a boil. A new recipe – boiled in hot water deli pressed turkey – ha, ha – made myself laugh. How do you get this bag off?"

I looked down at this purchased turkey-lump: "You don't look like much – all five pounds of ya! Must have been a sick one. I didn't know that they grew them this small. Should have read the fine print on whatever came with this bird – I guess it's a bird – could be an opossum."

After the dinner struggle, I turned on the television to watch the parade – a lot of happy faces and excitement. Then came a few football games. I guess watching guys tear off another's helmet and stomping on it relieves tension. The fans in the stands liked it – they slapped hands and high-fived one another. Heck, I used to play football myself. And I liked the pileups and the biting and pinching that goes on in that entanglement of arms and legs. I just had to be careful not to bite my own leg. "Ha, ha – made myself laugh again."

Next on the holiday agenda: Time for a short snooze and then what everyone waits for: Dessert – hot coffee, pecan pie, pumpkin pie, and whipped cream. With all that exercise I witnessed today on television, I worked up an appetite. "Hey, how about a bourbon to settle the stomach? That'll hit the spot!"

Sipping my bourbon, I settled into my lousy rocking chair to wait out the rest of the day. Being alone for the holidays, I frequently talked to myself: "Another Thanksgiving Day gone by and nobody missed me. My new friend from yesterday, Paul, did invite me but I turned him down. I didn't want my drooping eye-bags to spoil his family's fun. So, humbug to me, old scrooge!"

But, to my wondering ears, the phone started to make noises like I was being texted or it could be that the house was on fire – I never could figure out this new technology. Yes, it really was a text and all I had to do was read it out loud to myself before the screen went dark. "I've got to find out what all those apps mean."

The text message: "Dad, we missed you today. Just wanted to let you know that we love you no matter what. Happy Thanksgiving. Lynn, Niki, Jamie, Aaron, and Mom, too!"

"Wow, this is some surprise. This turned out to be a better-than-expected Thanksgiving Day. But something is still missing – let me think." Then, it dawned on me what I had forgotten: How about giving a little thanks – it wouldn't hurt, you know!

"Sing unto the Lord, O ye saints of his, and give thanks at the remembrance of his holiness. For his anger endureth but a moment; in his favor is life: weeping may endure for a night, but joy cometh in the morning." Prov. 30.

Chapter Nine

"Father Drake – Friar Tuck – St. Gabriel"

Gabriel means "man of God." He is the most well-known angel to appear in Scripture. Each time he is mentioned, we see him act as a messenger to impart wisdom or a special announcement from God.

"And the angel answering said unto him, I am Gabriel, that stand in the presence of God; and am sent to speak unto thee, and to shew thee these glad tidings." St. Luke 1:19.

It was Friday morning. I checked my appointment book. The rest of the day was clear, as usual. It was still way too early for my type of client to be calling. They usually don't wake up until late afternoon and just in time for a smoke and a chug of the spirits. After what I've been through lately, I was of thirst for a shot myself. "Where did I put that bottle of who-shot-John? Wait, I need to see Father Drake. I need to know: what was that Clown person?"

My rude nemesis hanging on the wall: "ring, ring, ring, ring, ring, ring, ring!" I eased up after those 7 chirps and picked up the receiver. I paused just a second to gather myself with a deep breath. I was afraid that it might be someone who "used to be dead" named The Employer or The Clown. But I took a chance: "Hello, this is Riffle, may I help you?"

"Eddy, this is Father Drake. We need to talk. First, you need to upgrade your phone system to the latest technology – I can't text a wall dinosaur. Second, last night I had a meeting with a very interesting and mysterious person, and it left me bewildered. Can you stop by the church – preferably today? I think that it's urgent."

"Sure, Father Drake." (I was glad that he called. I needed information, but I didn't want to let him in on too much). "I have a client meeting this afternoon and maybe go get a new walkie-talkie. So, I'll stop by on the way about noonish. Won't take too long, will it? I'm awful busy with work. There's a lot of sin stuff going on out there right now and they need my legal common-man expertise. What you're preaching to them ain't sinking in."

"Just get here on time. I need to prepare my Sunday sermon about you."

Not being sure of what was going on in Father Drake's mind, I could not prepare myself about what to talk about except my past and I just want that forgotten. But I respected him so I made my way to the church. When I opened the huge entry doors, I found Father Drake sitting in the front row of pews. He was looking up at a couple of statues. He had a soft expression on his face – you know, the kind of look that makes you feel warm and cozy, if you are in the mood. "Well, I was not in the mood and not sure about opening up about all my problems!"

"Eddy, I'm glad you came. Sit here beside me and let's talk."

"Father Drake, I must admit this is a bit unusual. I come to church services sometimes but I'm not involved in much, no choir, no committees, no calling, not much help I'm afraid. You do know that I'm a deacon in the Church of Christ, but long ago and now inactive – lost my way. So, with all of that, what can I do for you? And, by the way, who are those statues that has your attention?"

"Those images are of St. Michael and St. Gabriel. I look at them while I meditate or have a need. They remind me that they are angels of heaven but have earthly duties to perform. Eddy, I also have duties and this morning you seem to be the task. For some time now, I've tried to counsel you about your self-inflicted low esteem and how you torture yourself and how you have turned your back on your beliefs. It's very clear that you are not progressing out of the 'I'm to blame' mode and have regressed into the 'I need more punishment' mode. And, I've had a visitor. It was last night and concerns you."

"You are right as rain, Father. I am what I am and I have no one to blame but me. It haunts me day and night. I'm having these awful nightmares and they are violent and getting worse. Sometimes I wish they would just come for me and get it over with! I need to pay the price."

Father Drake put his hand on Eddy's shoulder: "I was working last evening when the big church doors opened and in walked someone I had never met before. He looked peculiar because he was dressed in a brown robe that looked to me like Friar Tuck – like in Robin Hood movies. He also had a rope tied around his waist that he used for a belt and he carried a walking rod which had a hypnotic beam of light for its tip. When looking at that glow, I felt calm and under its influence – it was a strange feeling. He said that his name was not important and that he was not here for a confession but to deliver a message. What's more intriguing about the whole thing is that you, Eddy Riffle, was the center of his dialog. So, I just sat and listened and he did all the talking."

Eddy spoke up: "I know all about that light trick, but keep going, Father. What did this sackcloth have to say about me? You have my undivided attention – sorry about the pun."

"He basically told me to do my job and help you because you are not able to help yourself – except in the sass department. He said that you have lost the presence of the Holy Spirit in your life. This vacuum has been filled with other attitudes. Further, he said that you are generally a good and fair person – except for a little over charging now and then. And now you have become spiritually lukewarm and are not grasping the fullness of God's grace."

Eddy could only muster a meek reply: "Not sure where this is going, Father!"

"Well, to put it simply: You can't forgive yourself for many things. But God will forgive you if you repent. In the old testament time, King David of Israel was guilty of adultery and murder and God forgave him of his sins because he sincerely prayed and ask to be forgiven."

"David's sin: Is not this Bathsheba, the daughter of Eliam, the wife of Uriah the Hittite? And David sent messengers and took her; and she came in unto him, and he lay with her; and the woman conceived, and sent and told David, and said, I am with child." 11 Sam. 11:3-5.

"David's murder: Set ye Uriah in the forefront of the hottest battle, and retire ye from him, that he may be smitten, and die." 11 Sam. 11:15.

David's prayer: "I acknowledged my sin unto thee, and mine iniquity have I not hid. I said, I will confess my transgressions unto the Lord; and thou forgavest the iniquity of my sin." Psalms 32:5.

"All of us are important to God. In the Bible, He used some of the worst sinners, like King David, to do his will. He has jobs waiting for all. This visitor arrived with a message and to convey it, he blessed me with the feeling that there is something special for you to do – just ahead and you should be ready to accept. But a warning: 'I will not open the windows of heaven and pour down upon you a blessing if there is not room in your heart to receive it.' Do you understand the messenger?"

"I think so, Father, and I'll try to figure it all out. I'll let you know next time I stop by and how it's going. I think I'll be alright now that we've had this talk. It's been a tough road but I'm ready for my soul to unburden itself. I'll kneel tonight and ask. But, answer me this: Why so much attention directed at me? I'm just a simple-minded nobody, a common person that's just trying to survive. Why would God or even Friar Tuck waste the time?"

"I'm not sure what's going on, Eddy. But it could be a sign of some sort. Take it as a blessing. One thing for sure, if it is not a blessing, then it must be a warning! Or, maybe there is a job for you to do – a calling. God uses all of us to do his will especially those with willing hearts. We all have different talents and He must see something in you that the rest of us are missing, ha, ha! But, no joke, God knows all about Eddy Riffle and also all about The Deacon, so don't be stubborn."

"Not sure about all of that stuff, Father, but thanks for the concern. It's a mystery to me. I must go now – it's time for my client meeting." I was sorry that I had to tell a fib. I really didn't have a client meeting but I needed an escape excuse. Getting up to leave and under my breath, I whispered: "Sorry, Father, but I'm getting the creeps. Friar Tuck, no less! No calling for me. I have no talents!"

Father Drake shook my hand: "See you later and Merry Christmas. That's tomorrow, so say your prayers and come for services."

I thought: "That helped a lot. All I need is another lonely holiday!" My nerves were now totally frayed and firing on all cylinders like a flock of chickens running in all directions while evading the hatchet. When and where would the ax fall? "And on my deserving neck?"

From Father Drake a little wisdom as he walked Eddy to the door: "Our conscience is but a thin veil that separates right from wrong; as a spider's web that's so easily shattered by the breath of an urge. Once a desire is devoured, it becomes flimsy deceit with an elusive repentance longed for like salve for an itch. Peace of mind will not come by mere wishing. Can a tattered web or conscience be mended? Little child, put your footsteps in His and follow the path to The Shield; He will not deceive you."

Getting into my car, I could only think: "Why for me? God and I are strangers and how does he know about The Shield?"

Chapter Ten

"Christmas Eve"

"For I was an hungred, and ye gave me meat: I was thirsty, and ye gave me drink: I was a stranger, and ye took me in: Naked, and ye clothed me: I was sick, and ye visited me: I was in prison, and ye came unto me." Matt. 25:35-39.

It's been a month since Thanksgiving Day and both Eddy and Ellie are emotionally ready to reconcile. What's holding them apart? Sometimes it might take that one right moment, or that one right happening, or that one right sparkle of the eye.

"Hey, Mister, Move Over a Little Bit!
It's Crowded Tonight."

It was Christmas Eve and Eddy was alone to soak in his misery. No place to go and no one who cared. Since Thanksgiving, Ellie had been hinting that she was ready to forgive but she still had the vision of Aebra on her mind. So, he walked the city streets hoping the lights and the bustle of people still doing their thing would bring him needed solace. It was soon evident that he would not find comfort this night. Traffic was light because most people did not celebrate Christmas out in the open anymore. It was because of friction and harassment.

Eddy was wandering aimlessly when suddenly a brightly lit nightclub blocked his passage. "Might as well go inside and see if I can find some Christmas cheer — the wet kind. I'm getting nowhere out here alone in this obnoxious and scary-acting crowd."

Inside the establishment, there were gangs of people that seemingly knew everybody in the place. There was dancing, laughing, drinking, and plenty of noise making. But no matter what Eddy tried, he could not find a friendly soul that would offer a smile or a nice hello. Most just wanted to know if he had a spare joint.

Eddy obtained a frozen drink of some sort and sat by himself at a booth where he could look out the front window. He watched the people coming and going. Not very exciting but it was something to do on Christmas Eve. Then, the front door opened and in proceeded the "down and out" folks — it was the usual time for the homeless and castoffs to arrive and make their plea for eats.

The manager scurried over and cuddled his arms like a shepherd tending a flock of sheep: "Go to the back door and hurry — it's unlocked. There's a room there. Go on in and I'll be right with you. I'm full tonight and I don't want you to scare off my crowd. And I don't want them to know that you are here – they frighten easily – they live in another world."

Eddy saw this as an opportunity for companionship and joined the vagabonds around to the back. The manager soon appeared and began a process of distributing bags of foodstuffs to eagerly waiting hands. Eddy received his bag and then settled down with the others. The manager then announced that all would be allowed to congregate in that back room where there was plenty of water and other necessities. And, they were able to stay all night if they wanted. As he said: "It's Christmas Eve, Merry Christmas!"

Before the manager left to attend to his business needs, Eddy asked him: "Why did you do this act of kindness?"

The manager responded: "It's the least that I could do considering the example. It's the one that says:

'For I was an hungred, and ye gave me meat: I was thirsty, and ye gave me drink: I was a stranger, and ye took me in: Naked, and ye clothed me: I was sick, and ye visited me: I was in prison, and ye came unto me.'" Matt. 25:35-39.

After many hours of talking with the multitude of homeless, helpless, and destitute, Eddy realized his personal misery was not alone but had plenty of company. So, he decided to spend the rest of the night with his new and only friends. The lights went out and everyone found a place to stretch out and it was somewhat crampy.

"Hey, mister, move over a little bit! It's crowded tonight."

It wasn't the Christmas Eve that Eddy wanted but it might have been the one that he needed. And, maybe it was one that The Deacon needed!

Chapter Eleven

"The Fight with Michael on Christmas Day"

"And Jacob was left alone; and there wrestled a man with him until the breaking of the day."

It was Christmas Day and for The Deacon, solitaire was the only game in town. It would be a Christmas to remember;

As the day passed, I conceded that it was a blue Christmas without you and decided it was time for a merry nip. After a few sips, I was singing: "You ain't nothing but a burned-out old flop-eared dog leading Santa's sled on a foggy night with a wet nose." Maybe my song words were off but the message was clear. My mood: "It's going to be a long day. And, it was!"

It was not yet midnight and another Christmas Day was dragging to a close. I made my way to the coffee pot for a stabilizer. "No sleep or merry dreams tonight. I'll just stay awake and play more solitaire or something."

Outside I heard a noise. Sounded like a "whinny snort." It's was a horse sound. "What would a horse be doing outside my window at midnight? That's it – reindeer! Maybe it's Santa Claus and he's making late deliveries."

I made my way over to the window and opened the sash. I peeked out and yes, it was a horse. A black horse and he was indeed stomping, snorting and whinnying. It looked like a horse that I had seen before. It was like the one that Michael rode when he paid me that surprise visit. He said that he would be back. But this time: "I'm not going to be taken so easily. He's in for a Christmas surprise. So, let him come!"

The best place to hide was behind the file cabinet beside the office door. It was dark and he would have to take a few steps inside to see anything. "I'll jump him and beat him senseless. Maybe angels have a glass jaw!"

Crouching, I could see the front door. I focused on the knob. It started to twist slowly. I held my breath and told myself: "Be still my thumping heart. I must not make a sound. I can't give him any advantage."

It was quiet – really quiet. Then, a sudden burst with a foot that flung open the door. "Ta-ta. So, they call you Eddy! Are you there?"

I gave no response and remained poised for an attack. My hands began to twitch, warning me that I was lapsing into the past. I was helpless to deny my brain. Then, the shadowy figure inched further into the office and toward the back room where I surely was sleeping. A few more steps and I would pounce. I have done this many times before: "We'll see if this intruder can take a good round-house punch to the chin and then a karate chop to the jugular vein."

The time was right. I stood up and leaped. Landing on my target's back, we both went sailing over my desk and onto the floor. I got my first view and all my fears were accurate. "It was Michael and he was not a happy angel!"

Time was lost as we struggled in the darkness – my trance and military training against his angel training. Tables, chairs, lamps, cabinets, everything was busted in the endless wrestling. No quarter was given. Hours passed and my strength was waning. I knew that I could not relent or he would take my soul. I also figured that he would not quit or even give an inch because to do so would be failure for his heavenly mission.

My last bit of energy has entered blast off mode. We were chest-to-chest, face-to-face, and breath-to-breath. It was a dead-heat, so far. I was about to yell "uncle," when the morning sun began to peek through the torn curtains that barely hung. What a mess a little scuffle can make of a business office. As we rolled about, my attention was drawn to a hanging mistletoe that only possessed one bead – all alone – on the last twig. It precariously dangled from the doorframe as if refusing to drop without receiving at least one lasting sincere kiss. Then, a revelation: "Is that mistletoe sending me a message that I'm still hanging by that single hair of horse's tail and doomed without a kiss from my love, Ellie?"

We both was near exhaustion when sunlight began to lighten the mess of my office. Michael halted and looked at me with his wide-open eyes. It wasn't hard to see me because we were almost eyeball-to-eyeball. Then, he released his grip just long enough to speak: "Let go of me – for the day breaks."

Not about to waste my opportunity: "I will not release you until you admit that you did not prevail against me and you will not take my soul until I'm good and ready. Do I have your word on this?"

Michael had a strange look: "Once before this occurred. It was a long time ago to a fellow named Jacob. What happened back then set a precedence that is recorded in the Holy Scriptures. Today, I thought Christmas would be a good time to remind you whose birthday we should be celebrating and how this blessed event is part of your mandate. I will acknowledge that we have wrestled all through the night and I have not, nor at this time wished to, prevail against you – after all, you are The Deacon.”

We then released each other from the strangle holds. Michael did not say another word, eased up and then departed. I rushed over and peeked out that beat-to-a-pulp window, I could see Michael gingerly mounting that black horse and poof they were gone. “I guess I messed up his Christmas and maybe mine also. Wow, even he knows what my army buddies once called me – amazing!”

I sat down and rested from my ordeal: “No use trying to sleep now and I’ll have a time cleaning up what looks like a bachelor party.” Lamenting: “I still have an office to run today and I sorely need some cash. And to beat all, I might have to replace this lousy rocking chair!” Then, my foggy brain reminded me that I must check out that Bible story.

“And Jacob was left alone; and there wrestled a man with him until the breaking of the day. And when he saw that he prevailed not against him, he touched the hollow of his thigh; and the hollow of Jacob’s thigh was out of joint, as he wrestled with him. And he said, let me go, for the day breaketh. And he said, I will not let thee go, except thou bless me. And he said unto him, what is thy name? And he said Jacob. And he said, thy name shall be called no more Jacob, but Israel: for as a prince hast thou power with God and with men, and hast prevailed.” Gen: 32:24-28.

“You know this Jacob guy stood his ground and because of his sincere heart, he was labeled a prince and was eventually made the father of Israel. How does that affect me?”

Then, I caught myself: “What about my check for 15k?” I had forgotten to wrestle it back from Michael. “I bet it was right there in his front pocket all the time. Next time for sure, Michael!”

From the Author:

He that hath a forward heart findeth no good. Prov. 17:20.

Eddy faces "hatred and adultery." He just plain loathes Aebra Arlington. She was one of the reasons for his guilt complex. It was so consuming, he refused to forgive himself for his adulterous thoughts and actions and actually had imposed self-punishment and sorrow. This path did not diminish his suffering. Fate presented Eddy with this unique opportunity to reap total, lasting and satisfying vengeance upon his accuser and temptress. "It was time for pay back!"

"An angry man stirrith up strife, and a furious man aboundeth in transgression. A man's pride shall bring him low; but honor shall uphold the humble in spirit." Prov. 29:22-23.

Chapter Twelve

"Aebra Arlington's Trial – The Truth"

Aebra was still Triple AAA and I was again stricken by her beauty. I tried to hide the battle that was going on inside my heart and my brain. But, I could not and would not let my temptation win. "Besides, I need to pay her back, big time!"

Ring, ring, ring, ring, ring, ring, and ring again trumpeted that menace hanging on the wall. I was beginning to dread the sound of that phone. It brought me nothing but consternation, fear, worry, questions and you-name-it. In a disgusting tone: "Hello, this is Eddy Riffle, attorney and private investigator. How may I be of service?"

"Mr. Riffle, this is the county clerk of courts and this is just a reminder that your court date with the Honorable Judge Grace R. Rule is scheduled for 2:00 P.M. today."

"Oh! O.K., thank you, I'll be there." The Honorable G. R. Rule (I think that GR should stand for grrrrrr) is about to use me again as a public defender for one of those Florida saps I keep mumbling about. Right now, I'm on good grounds with the judge after that A. Baddon bust, but I still have to take her cases just to get a few favors.

At the courthouse talking with the judge: "Mr. Riffle, I appoint you as public defender for the state's case against Ms. Aebra Arlington who is charged with blackmail and making false allegations. Are you prepared to accept this position?"

I was shocked and could not believe my ears: "Yes, your honor, but I think that I ought to tell you that I know this particular Aebra Arlington. I used to work at the same law firm. Maybe you should pick someone else for this case. I don't know if I can be impartial and give this defendant a proper defense. And, she's got plenty of cash so why a public defender?"

"Preliminary hearing is set for next Monday. Do your best and remember your oath to this court, so do your duty. If you need more time, please inform me via the clerk of courts. Good day, Mr. Riffle. Oh, by the way, she asked for you."

I thought: "Man-o-man, am I going to fix her wagon! But, why ask for me? What's she up to? Why not get one of her fellow stooges to do the job? I better get her story now!"

City Jail: I was sitting at the desk when the officer and the defendant entered the room. Aebra looked at me with those beautiful blue eyes. She had a slight tear in her eye that was hugging a lash about ready to fall. I handed her a tissue from the box on the table.

"Here, Aebra, there's no crying in jail. Besides, it might give the impression that you are innocent and we both know that's not the case. But, sit down and tell me what this is all about. Would you mind if I called you Delilah, like in Sampson?"

"Eddy, I guess I deserve that, but let me tell you how much I regret what happened to you at the firm. I've made mistakes, big mistakes. But, now that's all in the past. I want to make it up to you and you know that I'm able and willing. If you can just save my career and get back the position that I lost at the firm, I will clear you of those past silly accusations. And, we can be close friends again, if you know what I mean?"

Aebra was still a very alluring woman and I was again stricken by her beauty. I tried to hide the battle that was going on inside my heart and my brain. But, I could not and would not let my temptation win. "Besides, I need to pay her back, big time!"

"You mean, I take your case, win the case in court, arbitrate for you at the firm, and then get your close attention for payment. How neat is that? Aebra, I was a moron once but never again. If I defend you and get you what you want then I want only one thing and it's not you, nothing personal. I respect your expertise but you must tell my wife that you are an ambitious strong woman and that you set me up so I would be axed and out of your way. Also, you will tell her that I did not have a relationship with you. We were only laughing friends having after work drinks for stress relief. Is that a deal? And in writing!"

"Eddy, Mr. Riffle, it's a deal!"

Later at the Tampa Law Library: I was having a difficult time preparing Aebra's defense because I thought that I really hated her for what she had done to my life. Books and notes were scattered all over the library table. Down at the other end sat a young man trying to study: I spoke to him just to break my writer's block.

"Studying for the bar exam?"

He looked up, "Yea, it's a bear of a test but I'll make it. Nothing worthwhile comes easy. You an attorney?"

"You might say so but my clients have different opinions. It's never open-and-shut like in the movies. Each case is different and this one has me personally involved. I can't justify to myself the required defense because of personal involvement with my client. I don't want to bore you with the details. Say, what's your name?"

"My name is Ben. May I offer a suggestion? My professors taught us to always be ready with advice, preferably the kind that pays money. I don't want to seem impertinent being that you are already an attorney but it might be good to get another perspective."

"Sure, go ahead, Ben, it can't do me any harm."

"Well, it's kind of a golden rule that I've used in my young life. My father, also an attorney of sorts, taught it to me and it has passed the test of time."

I personally didn't think that I would ever use a student lawyer's advice or suggestions, but I liked this boy so I thought that I would humor him and listen. "Let's hear what your father taught you and go from there."

Ben closed his study manual and reached inside his pocket and pulled out a laminated index card. By the sight of it, I could tell it was well read. He began:

"These six things doth the Lord hate: yea, seven are an abomination unto him: A proud look, a lying tongue, and hands that shed innocent blood, An heart that deviseth wicked imaginations, feet that be swift in running to mischief, A false witness that speaketh lies, and he that soweth discord among brethren." Proverbs 6:16-19.

"Mr. Riffle, these passages probably fit your clients but they are not only for them – they are also for you. If you exhibit any of these inclinations and fall short in doing your best then you will never amount to anything. That's my father talking to me and to anyone listening. Also, you will fret the rest of your life. So, get in the habit of doing the right thing!"

Ben put the index card back into his jacket pocket and then lit his face with a big smile. "Got to go, tomorrow is my big test and I need my rest. See you in the courts, Mr. Riffle. Hope we are on the same side. If not, take it easy on me."

As I watched him leave the library, I had but one curious thought: "I never told him my name. How did he know my name was Mr. Riffle?"

The trial lasted about three weeks and was testy. I put all my effort into the case. I wanted Aebra's confession to Ellie. Also, the advice that Ben, or his dad laid on me, weighed heavily in my decision to be professional and honestly defend her.

In court, I was able to prove that one of the law firm's partners, Mr. Wigime, was infatuated with Ms. Arlington and made advances. The proof of this premise was neatly stored in his office personal computer which contained emails, notes, etc. that had no acceptance or replies from Aebra. The evidence supported the defense that he did, in fact, make advances (induced or not) and then tried to hide it by firing her. When Aebra made accusations and filed charges with the firm, Mr. Wigime claimed that he paid her blackmail with cash and promotions because she threatened: "I've had people fired before!" In retaliation, Mr. Wigime, used his position and influence to have her arrested and charged with blackmail. His evidence for his charges contained vague records of cash payments and his own personal diary which included ambiguous events, dates and circumstances. While on the stand, I made him look like a sniveling pervert – "Sorry, but everything goes in court."

After deliberation, Judge Rule's decision was for the defendant, Aebra, and dismissed all charges against her. I personally am not 100% sure that the partner was guilty but it sure looked that way. But, then again, I did too! Subsequently, in the settlement, the law firm agreed to a severance package that Aebra was very pleased with. But this time she had to leave the firm, quietly.

Judge Rule spoke to me after the trial on the front steps of the courthouse. "See, Eddy, that was not so hard." She turned and continued on down the steps. All I could manage to think of was: "Hey, Judge, when do I start getting paid?" She just laughed.

As for my honesty, my former Tampa law firm was impressed and apologized for believing the wrong person. And, they congratulated me on a very professional trial and that I was able to put aside any personal motivations for revenge against my client. To show their remorse for their own hasty actions, they contracted to me a junior partnership with a nice financial package. I accepted, of course.

My compensation from Aebra was simple: "Meet with Ellie and confess." Aebra is very convincing, so she will have no trouble emphatically telling the truth. Hopefully, if she follows through, this will finally take her out of my life. I promise not to hate her guts; like I do now.

Chapter Thirteen

"Valentine's Day"

At Eddy's place: Another holiday to help my mood. Who invented all these days of cheer and merry-making? Why not a day for deadbeats and losers and the woe-is-me people? If I went down to the city dump, maybe I could join in the party. "Hey, I got the nachos!"

At Ellie's place: The doorbell rang and to Ellie's surprise, it was a deliveryman with candy and roses. There was a card attached. *To: Ellie – Just to let you know that I never stop thinking about you. My love is forever and I'll always be close, if needed. Eddy.*

Ellie was touched by such a loving thought and was beginning to question herself about their separation. Was it now time to forgive?

About an hour later, the doorbell rang once again. Ellie did not know the young lady who was visiting. "Hi, my name is Aebra Arlington. I worked with your husband at the Tampa Law Firm. Do you have a few minutes? I would like to talk a while – if you have time."

"Sure, come on in. I have some hot coffee. Would you like some?"

"Why, yes, I think I might need it!"

After a few minutes of chitchat about unimportant things, Aebra got to the point. She told the whole ugly story and about what did not happen. She came clean. She spilled the beans. She was the goose that needed to be cooked. She kept her part of the bargain. Eddy won her case in court and now she was paying the fee.

After Aebra left slightly sobbing, sincere or not, Ellie decided to call Eddy. It was a very good Valentine's Day!

Chapter Fourteen
"Welcome Home, Eddy"

I rummaged through an old and dusty pile of documents and papers that used to be important to me but over time had lost their luster. "Ah, here it is – I hoped I had not thrown you away." When I was active and serving as a deacon, I used this very paper to help answer that question:

"How do I pray?"

It was about noontime when I was awakened by that irritating phone on the wall that blasted out once again: Ring, ring, ring, ring, ring, ring, and ring! If it wasn't so old, I'd hammer it! "Hello, this is Eddy."

"Hi, Eddy, this is Ellie. Are you busy?"

"Ellie, is there something wrong? Are Niki and Lynn and the kids alright?"

"Yes, we're all O.K. I just need to talk to you. A fellow attorney of yours came to see me. Her name is Aebra Arlington. She told me everything. I now know that I was wrong for not believing in you and for not being more trusting. I shared her information with the girls and they teared up and thought that you should come home."

Ellie with quivering voice: "Now I have you on my mind and I just wanted to hear your voice. It seems that the reason we are separated is not that important anymore. I don't know where to start. I'm sorry but I thought that you ought to know."

"Ellie, honey, you don't know how much I have wanted to hear those words. Without you, I haven't felt well or been myself ever since that awful day. My soul is tired and weary with the guilt I carry. It seems so long ago that I failed my family. I thought I had lost you forever. Can we meet for dinner tonight and make some family plans? Bring the girls and the kids and the dads – all of them, if they can come."

"Yes, pick me up at eight o'clock. I'll ask the girls – they will be so happy."

I hung up the phone and put my hands over my face because I could not hold back the tears. The great burden that was hounding me has just been lifted. I thought: "If my family was willing to forgive me, then I could forgive myself, just as Father Drake suggested. If I want to be happy again, I must forgive myself and that's final!"

Slowly, I made my way up the driveway to the front door. I was dressed in my last pressed shirt and somewhat clean everything else. I practiced what I would say to her when she opened the door, but everything was now a blank. "Just go for it," was my last muttering before the ringing of the bell.

"Ellie, my love." That was all I could get out before the hugs and kisses. Parting for a second: "It's been so awful without you. I'm so sorry. I want you to know that I will do anything to rid this wedge between us. I want my family back!"

Without speaking, Ellie took my hand and led me inside where the girls and all the family were waiting. They rushed me and threw their arms around me and we all hugged. I was overcome with emotion because I knew I was loved and forgiven. After much sweet talk and catching up, we all left for dinner at our favorite restaurant. I was a happy man again and my pride was beaming – I was with my family!

At the restaurant, at the table, the waiter approached. He was a tall, slender, nice-looking fellow with a thin mustache and eyebrows that matched. His eyes looked soft and tantalizing in a mysterious way. I thought: "What a pleasant face. If ever I wanted to be hypnotized, he could do the job."

Without waiting for me to speak, the waiter said, "My name is Angelo and I'm filling in for a friend tonight. And, let's start by saying: What a nice family we have to brighten our establishment. It will be a pleasure to serve. I hope you enjoy your evening and that your intended purpose will be fulfilled. I will try to make your experience with us 'one you will always remember.' I have prepared a special treat with your favorite delicacies. Enjoy!"

I looked at Ellie and she looked at me. We were both pleasantly surprised at what we had just heard from the waiter – it was as if he knew of our situation and was happy for us! And all evening we received the grand treatment with great food and close attention to our every need – even three fellows played the violin right by our table – without us asking.

Angelo was a perfect host and surprised us: "To the Riffle family, I would like to propose a toast to a new beginning." With glasses of water raised: "May your love and happiness surround you and strengthen you for all eternity." He then gave us his last big smile that reflected a sparkle off a gold front tooth. He then said: "Gotta go – more chicken to fry!"

Eddy: "Wow, that was nice. And now for some more good news: I have my position back with the Tampa Law Firm as a junior partner. I will make enough to help send these 'rascals for grandkids' of mine to college when they're ready. And, maybe we can get that new house that we have always wanted with that swimming pool."

The entire Riffle family enjoyed a wonderful and emotional experience and they especially liked our surprise announcement: Ellie and I decided to have Father Drake remarry us and we would repeat our wedding vows. A date had already been reserved and afterward, we were going a honeymoon – just like the first time. We wanted to start anew and have it last forever. And, I could not see the bride before the wedding. The girls giggled when I sheepishly added: "The hard part is my staying away from mom the next few weeks, but the anticipation feels good and natural. It's good to be loved."

After the enjoyment of the family dinner, I went back to my office for some quiet thoughts and to dwell on what had just occurred. I sat alone in the darkness to think and to plan for the future. And, I wanted to pray – it would be my first sincere prayer in a long time. I still remembered how to pray but I had forgotten how to trust and have faith that my prayers would fall on hearing ears. Then I remembered a little box that I kept on the top shelf of my one and only closet.

I rummaged through an old and dusty pile of documents and papers that used to be important to me but over time had lost their luster. "Ah, here it is – I hoped I had not thrown you away." When I was active and serving as a deacon, I used this very paper to help answer the question:

"How Do I Pray?"

"But, thou, when thou prayest, enter into thy closet, and when thou hast shut thy door, pray to thy Father which is in secret; and thy Father which seeth in secret shall reward thee openly." Matt: 6:6.

"Therefore, I say unto you, What things soever ye desire, when ye pray, believe that ye receive them, and ye shall have them." Mark 11:24.

"Well, I am already in my closet, so maybe my Father is in here with me."

While meditating in this quiet time in the darkness, something told me that I must forgive Aebra or I would not feel God's blessings when praying. That barrier to God will not unravel if my heart is not sincere.

So, I phoned her (I quit calling her Triple AAA) and we had a nice talk with no yelling. We decided to put the past in the past and start anew – like two people who just met and without history. We decided to communicate once in a while and chat. She surprised me when she was even open to my Christian style of advice. She wanted to change her life. She realized that it was time to consider starting a family of her own and the happiness that it would bring. I called Father Drake and arranged for her a meeting. For now, she's in the need-to-seek stage. Good for her.

Chapter Fifteen

"High School Friend"

"I'm no angel, as you know! Besides, big and tough Eddy is scared. When it comes right down to it, I'm afraid that my name is not in the book – you know, the big book! And I think that Michael is helping to write that book."

At my local bookstore, I made my way down the aisle in the religious section. I needed some answers: "Who really is this Michael guy and what's his game?" As I was fumbling around and not getting any place, I heard in the aisle next to mine: "Let me help you, sir, I know where everything is located, even the comic section."

Parting the books and being surprised: "Faye Marlow, is that you?"

Faye was a high school classmate and past friend. It had been a long time since we last crossed paths. We used to keep in touch but drifted away. At the current time, I was in sore need of a friendly voice, so I was happy to see her smiling face.

"Faye, what a pleasant surprise. Do you work here?"

"Eddy Riffle, what a nice gift to see you. It's been a while and I was wondering where you were and what's you've been doing with yourself. Yes, I work here part time. You know me. I need to be around people."

"I sure do. Let's quit talking through this peep-hole and go sit at that table in the front so we don't irritate the good customers."

I hurriedly put the books back in place and made my way to the table. "Faye, I'm glad we bumped into each other. I do need to find something but I don't want to bother you with my situations."

"Why, Eddy, you have not been bashful before. You know that I will help you with anything. We could always confide in each other and in confidence. I can't count the times in our school years that you gave me advice that I appreciated. That's what old friends do for one another – help with care."

"I know, Faye. I do trust you. So, here goes my story and don't laugh. It's all true."

I told her everything from A to Z. My whole story about the war, about Aebra Arlington and my downfall, about Ellie and my daughters, and about Michael. Now, I needed to know the facts about Michael. Why was he pointing his attention in my direction and why was he wasting his precious time on useless me?

"Faye, I'm no angel, as you know! Besides, big and tough Eddy is scared. When it comes right down to it, I'm afraid that my name is not in the book – you know, the big book! And, I think that Michael is helping to write that book."

"Come on, Eddy, and quit whining, let's take a look and see what we can find. Maybe there is an answer that will allow you to be more trusting in the blessings that are there for everyone, not just for scared little Eddy. Let go look in the Pity section, ha-ha."

"You're a hard nut for a part-time book store clerk. So, let's get cracking. Get it, nut, cracking?"

Shirley knew exactly where to find the reference books and was adept at scanning the material. What we found was information clearly contained in Biblical scriptures. Michael is mentioned three time in the Hebrew Scriptures (Daniel 10:13-21). The prophet, Daniel, has a vision where he identifies Michael as an angel that is the protector of Israel. Daniel is informed in his vision that Michael will arise during the "time of the end."

"And at that time shall Michael stand up, the great prince which standeth for the children of thy people: and there shall be a time of trouble, such as never was since there was a nation even to that same time: and at that time thy people shall be delivered, every one that shall be found written in the book." Daniel 12:1.

Faye and I talked for a long time about what these verses indicate and how they might be meaningful to recent occurrences. It was getting late: "Well, Shirley, it's about time that I leave you to close up this place. I'm afraid that I took up too much of your business time. Will your boss be upset?"

"No, Eddy, my boss will not be upset. On the contrary, he is very pleased with how I have spent the afternoon with you. Knowledge is wisdom and will never lose its value. It will help you to make the right choices that are facing you. So, buck up and don't be scared of that name in the big book thing. You've had some rough and trying times that would undo most folks but not you. You're still kicking like a bucking bronco and braying like a stubborn mule."

"Aw, Faye, as they say: 'Don't stick your finger in the cage!'"

"Eddy, Eddy, I hate to leave but there's other things to do today. This has to be a short visit because I'm in big demand at this old library. It would fold up without my part-time help. If you ever need me or just want to talk, I'll be sitting here at this desk – it's my spot."

"I'm glad that I bumped into you today. See ya around, old friend – talk later."

I hugged her and left the bookstore. It had been a long time since our last meeting. It sure was a good break that we met because she really helped. The time went too fast. "Oh well, I will try next week to come back for another visit and then we can talk more about our fun times."

Later when Eddy returned, he discovered that the library where they met was never a library but had always been a toy store.

"Be not forgetful to entertain strangers: for thereby some have entertained angels unawares." Heb. 13:2.

At this point, Eddy has now regained his job, his faith and ability to pray again, his family's love, and his happy way of life. And, he wants to live and forget the past. What else is there to accomplish? Then, why is Eddy still fearing another face-to-face with Michael?

"What do I have to do to get my name and my loved one's names in the Book of Life? And, I'm just plain afraid of what they will say about me on the judgment day. What will my family and friends think about me then?"

For Eddy Riffle and all of mankind, it's the last piece of the puzzle.

"So shall it be at the end of the world: the angels shall come forth, and sever the wicked from among the just, Matt." 13:49.

Chapter Sixteen

"Easter Day – The Vision of Jesus on the Road to Golgotha"

Then, from around the bend, the crowd began to mingle with voices raising as if Jesus was near. I could hear a various array of sounds with different meanings. And, some were crying, some were laughing and jeering, some were shouting for Jesus to take charge and lead them. It was like all the emotions of mankind were somehow now present at the same time.

Mr. Patron

He looked like a bum to me because his clothes were frazzled and aged. He had a haggard face that gave the appearance of being well traveled.

He turned to me and spoke: "Hey, buddy, can you spare a dime?"

I worked all Easter morning when I suddenly realized that something was wrong: "I'm hungry!" My appetite was finally coming back after being lost for two years. And, I was really missing that great taste of the first bite on a stone-cold empty stomach. So, I rushed down to the local deli for a baloney and cheese sandwich. I found an isolated table because I wanted some peace and quiet while I enjoyed my renewed taste buds. Everything seemed perfect to me except there was no waitress in sight. The only person in the joint besides me was the counter man. The name on his shirt – Joe. He took my order and soon delivered the sandwich, hard-boiled eggs, and sweet tea that I was chomping at the bit to receive. "Hummm, it was quite tasty."

The waiter checked on me and dropped off the check and then slowly made his way to the kitchen leaving me by my lonesome. I sipped my tea while enjoying the quiet. Then the front door opened and another person walked in and made his way over to the counter and sat down. He looked like a bum to me because his clothes were frazzled and aged. He had a haggard face that gave the appearance of being well traveled.

He turned to me and spoke: "Hey, buddy, can you spare a dime?"

I was not taken back by his brashness because I could clearly see his condition. "Sure, man! Get on over here and sit in this spare chair. It's empty and needs a customer."

He waddled over and sat down: "Thanks, I'm hungry enough to eat the bark off a tree. I think I've already had that meal a few times. As a last resort, I come in here when everything else is exhausted and old Joe gives me a handout."

Old Joe must have heard his name mentioned because he suddenly arrived at my table. "Can I get you anything else mister, apple pie maybe? Say, Mr. Patron, when did you come in?"

Before the hobo could answer, I spoke up: "He just got here and I do need something: I would like for Mr. Patron to have anything he wants to eat and give me the tab." I took out my wallet and looked inside. All that I had was that $100 bill that I kept so I would never be broke and for emergencies. I guess this fit that situation. I reached the money toward the waiter and told him: "Give my buddy here the change."

Then Mr. Patron reached over and grasped my hand: "Thanks again, but I will decline your offer of such great benevolence and concern. You see, I'm just passing through and I have sufficient substance waiting at the next stop. Old Joe and I have known each other for a long time and we work together in service."

I was a little shocked: "Then, why did you come over to my table? Do I know you from somewhere?"

"Eddy, you don't know me, and I just wanted to chat. Maybe I can be of assistance to you."

"Hey, Mr. Patron, you know my name. Man, I don't mind telling you that this is strange. What service do I need?"

With all that was happening to me lately, I was beginning to get used to crazy things. So, I slid my chair backward just to give me some jumping up room. "You never know!" I quickly looked at the man to see his reaction. All he did was to lower his eyes for a moment and paused. He then raised them up to meet my stare. Immediately, I fell under his hypnotic trance and was unable to get up and run out of that deli like I was burning to do. It was no use, so I relented and let his trance take me to another state of mind.

For me, it was like being at the movies: "You sit back and watch. You feel all the emotions of the scene before your eyes but you know that you can't change the action. Yelling and screaming only irritates the guy sitting beside you, so don't yell and scream."

The scene before me was in the time of Jesus of Nazareth. What I saw was a great multitude of people that nervously rustled back and forth on the streets of the city. One man in the crowd said that he was awaiting the appearance of a captured Jesus. He said that he got there early so he could get a clear view of "The King of the Jews."

Looking at the people that lined the streets, it occurred to me by their actions that they did not know what to expect. One questioned: "Will he break his bonds and destroy the captors with a single blow or will he be exposed as a fraud and a liar?"

Another said: "How should he be remembered? Is he the Son of God or just an ordinary man of teaching?"

Then, from around the bend the crowd began to mingle with voices raising as if Jesus was near. I could hear a various array of sounds with different meanings. And, some were crying, some were laughing and jeering, some were shouting for Jesus to take charge and lead them. It was like all the emotions of mankind were somehow now present at the same time.

I paused my thoughts for a moment to prepare myself for what was about to happen. My worst fears paled to what I now faced. The dragging of the cross screeched at my very soul as if I were actually present and part of the horrible scene. There it was: Jesus struggling, then falling, and then being struck with whips and canes while trying to carry the cross upon his back. Someone in the crowd cried, "Where is thy power to deliver us?" Others in the crowd tried to help Jesus and carry the cross for Him but were pushed back. Soon, a man from out of the throng came forward and helped a weakened and weary Jesus carry His cross.

Closer Jesus crawled and then was seemingly dragged to where I was viewing. I instinctively reached out for His bloodied hand to try and help Him to his feet. As I looked down, it was then that I met Jesus for the first time. Our eyes met and it was at this very moment that I understood.

Time seemed to stand still and everything stopped moving as if I had plenty of time to dwell on the face of The Lord. His eyes were kind and loving eyes, not filled with hate for His tormentors nor filled with revenge. His eyes were hurting eyes that were filled with the physical pain that He bore. His eyes were strong eyes that would not waver until his appointed task was completed. His eyes contained every answer for every question. His eyes told me that He loved me and every person that ever lived and every person that will ever live.

Even though not one word passed between us, I understood. My creation as a human being with an eternal spirit was explained in that moment and I understood. I thought: "If only I could take your place, even for a while." But I knew it could not be so. The cup could not pass and Jesus must do this and I understood. Then, pushing the crowd aside, the brutal guards took Jesus and continued their onslaught down the road to Golgotha or "the place of a skull." My vision could not follow Him further.

"Now from the sixth hour darkness came over the land for three hours and then Jesus cried out with a loud voice, Eli, Eli, lamasabach-tha-ni? That is to say, my God, my God, why hast thou forsaken me? He soon yielded up the ghost. The temple vail was rent in twain from the top to the bottom; and the earth did quake, and the rocks rent; and the graves were opened; and many bodies of the saints which slept arose. And the centurion, which stood over him, cried out, 'Truly this man was The Son of God.'" Matt 27.

I awoke from my vision and faced Mr. Patron. I could not speak. He put his hand on my clasped hands and he spoke: "If every human being could have been on that road to Golgotha and looked Jesus in the eye, they would understand. What a wonderful world it could be. We would be more loving and caring. We would do all we could to help others. We would be thankful Christians. God's Holy Word tells us that someday all of us will be able to see the eyes of Jesus and kneel before Him. What a beautiful thought."

"And there shall be no more curse: but the throne of God and of the Lamb shall be in it; and his servants shall serve him: And they shall see his face; and his name shall be in their foreheads." Rev. 22:3-4.

My ability to speak returned: Why did you give me a chance to understand what was before me all the time? I have never been able to let go of my human desires and be fully committed. But now I understand that faith in Jesus is "The Shield" and that He protects us from all the fierce darts of evil.

The patron came closer: "It isn't me or Michael that is giving you the chance, it is Jesus, your Lord and Savior. We work for Him. Now, it's time for you to follow your heart."

Then, Mr. Patron got up from the table, made his way to the exit, looked back and smiled one last time. He said: "By the way, my name is Gabriel and I'm an angel. I deliver messages from God. See you on down the road." Then he left with a wave and a nod.

My mind was now in a relaxed mode. I was beginning to understand what Michael wanted of me. And in my mind, I reflected on Michael's visits and my visions. I could now see that I needed to forgive myself of my indiscretions and sins just as I had visualized that Jesus had forgiven me. Even on the cross where Jesus died, He said: "Father, forgive them; for they know not what they do." Luke 23:34.

As I left the deli, Old Joe tipped his hat to me and spoke: "Call anytime, Mr. Riffle, I'll be here. This deli never closes. And, Mr. Patron, err, I mean Gabriel, just lives around the corner, someplace close."

Chapter Seventeen

"The Murder"

"What Could Go Wrong?"

The alley was dark from end to end. A man stood beside trash receptacles located behind a pastry shop. He had his weapon drawn. He was ready for action as he waited for his victim. Down at the far end, another man entered. He cautiously sneaked his way through the dark. As agreed, each turned on a flashlight that would signal their presence. Both men then stood face to face. They were unaware that another set of eyes watched. No words were spoken. The lights were doused. They fired their weapons into the darkness. Both, unknowingly, missed their targets. A single shot from a hidden sniper's rifle penetrated his target. Roddy Shaw lay dead. The other man, Jonnie Riffle, fled. He did not know that he did not kill Roddy Shaw. The sniper did the trick! He had a night scope.

From Eddy: Happiness is a frame of mind that welcomes great joy into my life. I was exonerated by my accuser of harassment and justifiably reinstated at the law firm, with promotion. My family situation is healing. I'll be home shortly. I visited my Christian church. It's still there in service. They would be happy for my return – they miss my voice in the choir. My college buddy, Detective Lt. Sam Holler, wants to play golf with me, like old times. I don't have as many nightmares. I feel like I can make it this time, so what could go wrong?

I was busy trying to catch up on a big pile of paperwork when that phone on the wall started again – what now? Ring, ring, ring, ring, ring, ring, and ring! "Hello, this is Eddy Riffle."

"Eddy, this is Jonnie! No phone joking this time. I just checked our lottery ticket and man you better sit down – we won! I checked the numbers and we have them all."

"Jonnie, my favorite brother of all time, how much did we win?"

"It's about two million dollars each. I can't believe it. Finally, we got the cash to live like we want, financially anyway."

"Man, you got to be kidding! Are you double-sure?"

"This is no time to kid – we won, I checked already by phone."

"Wow, now I can pay off my girl's Ivy League college bills and give Ellie some peace of mind. It feels good, even great, to be sort of rich. Keep that ticket safe and I'll be right over. We need to hit the lottery office and get it recorded and then spread the good news."

Driving across town to my brother's place, I starting thinking about what I was going to do with all that money. Getting greed out of your system takes time and effort. I found myself replacing all the good in my brain with thoughts about a vice here and there. But the trick is to make such thoughts pass and not linger. It's difficult but it's a must-do. For me, it takes a crowbar but I'm managing to pry out those thoughts.

Pulling in the driveway, I was met by Jonnie and he was in a hurry. "Let's get out of here. Company is on the way and they know I have the ticket. I messed up and told my racing bookie that I hit a lucky streak and could pay off. I couldn't help it, he pressed me for what I owe to the syndicate, and I let the cat out of the bag. He knows about the four million bucks!"

Jonnie then jumped into the front seat and I drove away fast: "Looks like he would be satisfied to get what you owe him. Why is he chasing us?"

"He wants it all – at least a big share, for interest. That's the way his kind works. If they get a sap like me on the hook, they own him now and forever. Sorry, Eddy, but that's what it is and I have to deal with it."

I could see that Jonnie was scared, so I reached under my coat and pulled out my secret protection – my .38-caliber police-special revolver. "Here, take this! If we get to the lottery office and record the ticket then we're safe for the time being and your bookie will have to wait for his take. I have my 45 in my belt but these weapons are only for protection. I repeat: We are not going to use them! They are for show and self-defense only! It's against God's law to kill anyone needlessly. So, don't use that rod unless our lives are in absolute danger and no way out. That's an order, little brother!"

I drove fast but not reckless. I didn't want a police car chasing us because of a traffic violation. We arrived at the lottery office that was located in the middle of town. Plenty of people were milling around the streets plus a cop's deli hangout was located across the street. It was lunchtime. And, the police were partaking of the specialty – chili hot dogs.

We rushed into the lottery office and slapped down that ticket. Not sure about what to say when one turns in a four-million-dollar winner, we hesitated. "Yahoo!" was all that came out of my mouth and a "you betcha!" came from Jonnie. The clerk said she had heard it all before. She just wanted the winning ticket.

Luckily, I had my briefcase which contained all the forms needed to set up the necessary legal trusts and secure the winnings. My family was getting my money and no gambler was about to outsmart me. It didn't take long for all the paperwork, trusts, and certifications to be completed and we officially became safe millionaires. It was a case of rags to riches, poor-man to rich-man, and from pauper to prince. We were all those things except dumb man to smart man!

Gushing with joy, we headed outside that lottery office and right into a conflict of interest. We were going to keep our money and someone else wanted to take it. Jonnie's bookie and a few of his associates were standing beside their flashy cars and looked unhappy. "How you doin', Jonnie?" shouted the one who was obviously the boss.

Jonnie whispered: "His name is Roddy Shaw and he's the local Vegas money bookie and strong-arm man. He's nasty business when he wants to be. We better take it slow and easy. I owe him about $100,000 bucks but his interest rate climbs fast, too fast for my liking. He'll get his 100 Gs and that's all – no more interest."

"How did you get so far in debt to that rat? I guess you didn't pay attention to your big brother's preaching? After this is over, I'll punch your ears down some, but not much." We both snickered a little. We were always close – wrestling and silly bro stuff.

Jonnie yelled out: "I'm fair-to-middling, Roddy. But I know why you are here and it won't work. It'll take a few weeks for the dough to get here and then with all the taxes and whatnots, it will just be enough to pay you off – all 100 big ones! All I'll have left is some pocket change and track money. It's a case of take it or leave it. Is that a deal?"

Roddy was not amused with Jonnie's offer and reached for his pistol. His employees did the same. Jonnie and I did the same. There we all stood with weapons pointing at each other. No one flinched. Roddy Shaw knew that if he shot us, he would get nothing. Also, he correctly guessed that we would not shoot because we are not natural-born murderers, like him. So, we all stayed calm but itchy.

It became a classic standoff with no one having anything to gain by firing their weapons. We slowly put them back in their place of hiding. And, it helped that those police cars sitting at the deli were facing in our direction. "Thankfully, no one pushed the panic button!" Instead there was some loud yelling and some unnerving threats and innuendos. Jonnie and I felt a little safer because our newest buddies, the police, were now intently watching. With this in mind, we backed away and slid into our car knowing that this was not over. I was particularly worried about their warning concerning my family's health. That part had me bothered and feeling queasy to think about what could happen.

On the way home, Jonnie and I decided to lay low until the lottery office completed their requirements. The wire transfers and legal stuff needed to clear the banks. It was unpleasant to think about the consequences that might come from Roddy Shaw, but we had no choice. We had to be alert and ready for anything.

A few days passed and I heard nothing concerning the situation until I picked up the daily paper to read the headlines: "Man named Roddy Shaw, notorious Vegas business personality, killed in back alley shootout. He was shot one time and apparently died instantly. No suspects are in custody at this time. Police are investigating all clues."

"Brother Jonnie, what have you done?"

I busied myself by packing into boxes what little stuff that I actually owned. I wanted to get home to Ellie. Still, no word from Jonnie. I paced the floor, wrung my hands, prayed for his safety and hoped it wasn't him that committed that murder. It's not like him to commit such a thing unless he had no choice and was backed into a corner.

I had to take my mind off Jonnie, so I dove into a pile of unpaid bills – that ought to do it. "I just hope that Jonnie is alright."

This time the phone on the wall shook me: ring, ring, ring, ring, ring, ring, and ring! The rings were haunting because I could feel that it was bringing me bad news. "Hello."

"Eddy, this is Detective Sam Holler. I have some bad news. Your brother Jonnie was found dead and floating in the bay. Sorry, but there's no easy way to let you know. It appears to be gang related. I'd like for you to come down immediately for a statement. You are implicated but I don't know in what way. You can help us to sort out this whole mess."

I was shaken to the core. "My brother Jonnie is gone. Why did this happen? We just won all that money and just wanted to enjoy the fruits of lavish spending."

I collected myself and with a quivering voice: "O.K. Sam, I'm on the way."

Sam: "I'm sorry, buddy. Wish I didn't have to be the one to do this."

Down at police headquarters, Sam greets: "Eddy, brace yourself. I might as well come to the point. Your .38 police-special revolver was found on Jonnie's body. And, after ballistic tests, it was determined that this revolver was the same one that shot a hole in the back of a pastry shop. It was not used to help kill Roddy Shaw. Your brother missed."

Sam needed answers: "I knew right off that this was your weapon, but I don't know how Jonnie got possession. Also, the weird part: A single rifle slug actually killed Roddy Shaw. The markings are identical to the bullet that got The Employer. It came from a sniper's M24. The question is, who pulled the trigger? Were you involved? I have to ask. Do you need a lawyer? You have a right to have one present."

"No, Sam, you know that I'm a lawyer so I can represent myself. I must confess that I gave the pistol to Jonnie for self-defense. He was in mob trouble due to gambling debts and they were after him. You won't believe this next part: We won four million dollars in the lottery and Roddy Shaw was after the money. I don't know why or if Jonnie killed Roddy Shaw, but I guess that's what happened. The mob must have paid Jonnie back, I suppose. Now, I don't know if they are after me or not, or my family. I had nothing to do with the shooting. I could not do such a thing. I don't believe in sniper work – that's killing."

Sam would have booked me right then if he had any proof or any substantial reason to believe that I did a sniper hit. Then, he shocked me when he reached into his blazer pocket and pulled out an envelope. He paused and then handed it to me. "This is why I'm releasing you for the time being. It was sent to me from your brother and seems to exonerate you. It's a good thing that he wrote this note, or the circumstantial evidence would have jailed you for a long stretch. Also, the DA wanted to book you on charges but finally took my advice and is letting you go with her warning: Don't leave town! Don't give me a reason!"

The letter read: "Brother, I'm so sorry that I got you and your family involved with my gambling situation. After thinking it over, I felt that the only way to get you out of this mess was to work it out with Roddy Shaw. I met him alone in the alley. He drew first but I shot first. The rest will be in the papers. This letter is to inform whomever that Eddy Riffle had no part in the 'shooting' of Roddy Shaw. I did it on my own, in self-defense, and without anyone's advice. I'm solely responsible! Sorry, brother. I hope this clears you, at least legally. And, if the bookie's men contact you, show them this letter and maybe they will let you slide. If you are reading this then I must be gone for good. I goofed!"

I folded a copy of the letter and put in my pocket and was headed back to my office when I got this weird feeling to go check on my family and make sure that they were safe. And, they needed to know about Jonnie. Besides, the gamblers think that I had a part in this ordeal. They are probably after me.

I drove slowly down their street. My eyes were darting back and forth trying to see if there was anything unusual or out of place. I didn't notice anything alarming, so I parked in front of the house. I turned off the key, opened the door, and started up the driveway. Around the corner of the garage came several armed men.

One yelled: "So, you thought that you and your sap of a brother could get Roddy and get away scot free. It doesn't work that way! You must pay, and you will pay! You and your whole family will suffer the price – compliments of your former associate, The Employer! It's time to collect the rent!"

I became desperate: "Wait, I have this letter that proves I had nothing to do with Roddy Shaw getting shot!"

But it was too late and when I reached into my pocket for the letter, the gang reacted by raising their weapons with intent to shoot. I had no choice but to grab my .45 pistol. But something kept my finger from pulling the trigger. It only took an instant to realize that I would not shoot. I could not force myself ever again to take another's life even at the expense of my own.

I tried to jump behind my car. I heard the *tat, tat, tat* of rounds breaking glass. It was no use. Helpless, I felt the sting of bullets ripping my clothing and flesh and then everything went black as I closed my eyes   it's over!

Chapter Eighteen

"Eddy Near Death"

"Above it stood the seraphims: each one had six wings; with twain he covered his face, and with twain he covered his feet, and with twain he did fly." Isaiah 6:2.

"The effectual fervent prayer of a righteous man availeth much." James 5:16.

"What man is there of you, whom if his son ask bread, will he give him a stone? Matt." 7:9.

"Eddy Near Death"

Eddy Riffle lies shot and near death in Orlando Regional Hospital. Doctors stated on record that he should be dead. Shot several times by a gang of thugs, he somehow clings to life and just maybe dodged that fatal bullet. After extensive surgery, blood transfusions, and an all-out effort by medical professionals, hope clings to a last-ditch effort: "Prayer!"

What happened: Eddy got hit hard and went down! Lying in his own blood in his wife's driveway, he was in need of mercy because a hailstorm of bullets was ricocheting in every direction. Still conscience and with pistol in hand, he could have returned their fire but refused to shoot back. Without defense, he was headed for the morgue. But the would-be killers were abruptly halted in their assignation attempt – they could not complete their mission. A fierce and defiant angel appeared and defiantly stood between the assassins and their bleeding target.

The angel covered Eddy with his giant bulletproof battle wings preventing further damage. An imposing foe, the angel stood eight-foot-tall and had six wings of fluffy white. And in his hand, the angel possessed a fighting sword that flamed with fire and was swifter than the eye could follow. One by one the assailants attacked the angel but their bullets mysteriously missed. And for their efforts, they were either hacked or slashed until they lost what little nerve they possessed and fled. Many heads would have been severed that day if the angel had been vengeful but instead, he was merciful. Without his intervention, it would have been a disaster. The Riffle family was safely inside the house. It was Sunday and they were all together.

A helpless man's thoughts: "Here I am – lying in my own blood that's shooting from my body like a sieve. It hasn't occurred to me yet that my body is about to die – naivety, I guess. My stomach began to turn sour and my head started throbbing. I was losing it fast and my alarm button was pushed. I could not think. What's must I do? Nothing came to my frantic mind but hang on and hope for help."

The angel approached the fallen Eddy and placed his hands on the wounds and the severe bleeding subsided. He then gently stroked Eddy's head and called out his name. Eddy was awakened and painfully spoke: "Am I still alive? Are you an angel? You come to get me?"

The angel did not speak. He closed Eddy's eyes with his hands so he could rest because his wounds were severe and he would need a miracle to survive. He was barely alive when the ambulance arrived on the scene. He was transported to the hospital emergency entrance and into surgery. The angel left as mysteriously as he arrived. Hallucination or for real?

During treatment, that much-needed medical miracle occurred when Eddy stopped all bleeding just short of no return. But with the severity of the wounds and because of the blood loss, he developed a high fever and evolved into comatose. Doctors could not provide a guarantee that he would ever return to a conscious state. It could be that last straw!

Doctor Marsh, Eddy's surgeon, arrived at the waiting room: "Mrs. Riffle, your husband has developed a high temperature. It's very serious and he will remain in a coma while his body fights. I do not know how or why he did not bleed to death lying on your driveway. It was a blessing, for sure."

Ellie bending over Eddy in the ITC unit and talking to herself: "He looks so helpless, with all the tubes and wires and instruments. He has always been so strong and self-reliant. He's never been physically injured this bad before. I thank the Lord that he is still alive."

Eddy mumbles: "Ellie, an angel saved me and Bob a long time ago. He just saved me again. He's here now. He's over there. Do you see him?"

"No, honey, I don't, but it doesn't mean he is not there. I believe you."

Dr. Marsh enters the ITC: "How's our patient doing?"

"He seems to be a little disoriented. And why is he talking about an angel that he seems to know? He said that it saved him twice! Then he went back to sleep."

Dr. Marsh scratches his head: "It's hard to tell. His temperature must go down to normal levels first and then his visions should clear up. If he is willing to fight hard enough, he should recover. Probably there won't be any significant brain impairment but there is always a chance. But he might talk a little nonsense for a while because of the high fever. And, because of his condition, he could experience some whopper dreams. He could visualize things that are not there or talk about events that did not occur – like his angel visits. But it was a close call and we should be grateful that he survived. Right now, he is probably experiencing quite an ordeal."

"Thank you so much, doctor. We will go home and let him rest. Please, please call us when to come back. We want to be here when he wakes up. He will be so glad to see the girls and grandkids fussing over him. He will need our TLC."

Doctor Marsh reassures Ellie that he will do everything necessary for Eddy and that he should recover: "The nurse will be in touch with you when he starts to move around and makes signs of waking. To see his family is the best medicine for him, so you can rest assured that we will call you immediately when it's appropriate."

Before leaving, Ellie whispers to Eddy: "If love can make you live longer then you will live forever because that's how long I will love you. We all love you. Get well for us. We'll be back to take you home. Don't worry about anything except getting better. If you would like, we will go fetch that lousy rocking chair so you will be comfortable. That's if it doesn't fall apart in the moving. Hold on and don't give up. We won't be gone too long. I'll bring back the Bible and read to you. Nothing for us to do right now but wait and pray and give thanks."

Meanwhile: Lt. Sam Holler, The District Attorney, Tampa City Mayor and Judge G.R. Rule held a meeting to discuss recent events involving Eddy Riffle, Mr. A. Baddon, Roddy Shaw, a person known as The Clown, and possibly Detective Boone. The evidence indicated that an indictment was in order. But for now, just a subpoena. You can't question a potentially dying man that is comatose.

Chapter Nineteen
Eddy's Coma – Visitors

"It's like I'm a little ship in a glass bottle – they look at me but they can't reach me."

I looked up as I was being carted through swinging doors and I saw a sign: Intensive Care Unit. "Wow, this must mean that they have already patched me up. I didn't feel a thing. But, why are people talking about me and I'm answering them, but they can't seem to hear me. Even if I yell, they still talk to each other but not to me. It's like I'm a little ship in a glass bottle – they look at me but they can't reach me."

It's true that some people might experience supernatural hallucinations or visions when they are about to be collected by the Grim Reaper or in a coma. How about both?

It was late. No lights anywhere except on the monitors that track my vitals. If I kick the bucket, all the alarms will go off in rhythm. Suddenly they did. The nurses began to run. I yelled: "I'm fine, just some indigestion!" But they couldn't hear me because I'm in a coma. "What if they kill me trying to save me? Those electrical shocks hurt. It's a false alarm. I think that I just need a bedpan and an antacid! Oops, I was right!"

Later: My attention is drawn by the creak of my door. A woman enters. She is bathed in nice perfume. She leans over me and smiles at my helpless body. I know this woman – it's Aebra Arlington – Triple AAA! She wants to attack me. She fumbles in her purse and pulls out a knife. She has flipped and wants to stab me! Closer she draws, but wait – it's a tube of lipstick. She smears her lips and begins smacking. She grabs me by the ears – I'm dead. But, instead, she plants a big red-lipped kiss on my cheeks – both of them. She whispers: "Eddy, get well, you are in my prayers – that's right, you have converted me. When Ellie sees these lip prints, she will slap you back to your senses! You need a good jolt! O.K. Mr. Sampson?"

My good feelings about Aebra were short-lived when other hallucinating visions made the scene: I tossed and turned and couldn't get to sleep because the band kept playing and shaking my bed. And, then this loud-mouthed guy started singing out in the hallway. Suddenly, it got quiet. I strained my ears to hear the slightest drop of a pin. Nothing! Abruptly, the sound of a drum beating reverberated and made me jump! Then the door opened and in popped a head of black greasy hair and sideburns. I tried to speak but this figure of a man shushed me with this: "If they can make penicillin out of moldy bread, they can surely make something out of you, son – so get with it before it's too late!" Then, that head of hair ducked away.

"How do I wake up? Pinch me! Throw water on my face! Yell in my ear! Put smelly socks to my nose! Tell me my mother-in-law is here! Well, what then? I'm in a coma! Because of my medical situation, I'm supposed to have whopper dreams but like this? Come on, man!"

"I don't know if my Nurse Cranky is a real person or imagined but she can talk to me and I can talk to her." Here she is: "Mr. Riffle, you have someone here to see you. It's your brother Jonnie."

"Oh good, show him in. We need to talk. I thought that he was floating in the bay."

Jonnie and I chatted for a few minutes and I told him about my visions and what a relief it was to wake up and find out that everything did not occur as I remembered. I quizzed him about the shooting details. He had never heard of Roddy Shaw and has no gambling situation. He said he never had lunch money, much less money to throw away. And, we did not win the lottery. And, he can't even hold a pistol with that old football injury to his shooting hand. And, he's not dead because he was standing right in front of me, blabbing. He was full of life and as happy as a newborn pup! Then I lost connection and faded out. But I did hear him whisper that he would return and get that overbearing, leather belt-strapping nurse off my back!

I was feeling better because of Jonnie but I was getting nervous about who would visit next. I was right in the middle of the hit parade. "Yea, who is it?"

Nurse Cranky said: Ben is here. Do you know him?"

"Well, I only met him one time. It was in the law library. He helped with a problem that I was wrestling with."

Ben enters the room and makes his way over to Eddy. "How you doing, old timer? I heard that you had a close call but you're too mean to croak. I've been curious about your defense of Aebra Arlington. Did you win? Did you make the judge cry?"

"Yea, I won – you young squirt! Did you pass the bar exam?"

"Yes, sir, by flying colors, it was a snap. I had a lot of incentive to pass the tests and worked hard because I've been called to help others; like on missions that requires responsibility."

"Wow, good for you. It sounds important and you seem eager to start. Can you tell me what the mission is all about?"

"You might say that right now I'm doing some on-the-job training. It's like this: 'I was involved in a bad car accident when I was just a senior in high school – I barely survived but my parents were lost. My dad was driving but could not avoid the collision. My life was altered forever. I was left basically alone – no close relatives anywhere – just distant cousins. It hit me hard and I fell into deep depression – mentally and physically.'"

"Sorry, kid, I feel for you. I know all about depression. Don't let it get the best of you like it did to me. Just seeing you and how happy you have become gives me a big lift. But I'm puzzled. I thought that your father was still helping you with your law career and giving advice."

Ben wiped his eyes: "I will never forget the advice and instruction my earthly father taught to me and I call upon it every day to make decisions. But the advice I gave you in the library was from my heavenly Father. I was badly injured and lying in the hospital when the angel visited. It was a very pleasant experience and I felt like my dad was somehow accompanying him and even sat on my bed and patted my head. I was emotionally uplifted and felt that my dad was telling me that it was alright to listen to the angel. My dad somehow whispered to me that the angel was named Gabriel."

Eddy smiled: "I guess I'm not the only one that was blessed by Gabriel. I've been touched also. It took me a while to figure it all out, but now it seems so clear. And, this you won't believe. I was visited by another angel. His name is Michael. I was scared of him at first but now I feel comforted by his presence and what he expects of me. He's coming back for another visit; he told me so."

Ben with enthusiasm: "How about if I add more to the mysteries? As for meeting you in the law library, it was not by accident. Gabriel put thoughts in my mind that I might be able to help you with your struggle to defend Aebra Arlington in a court trail. Glad you listened!"

"Thanks, Ben. You did help me and best of luck with your future. Hopefully, you will have a long and successful life filled with many missions and endeavors."

"Thanks Mr. Riffle, maybe I just needed to hear your words. In some ways, you really resemble my dad; and not just because you're old as Methuselah. That's a joke! Well, got to go for now. I'll keep in touch because I trust your wisdom. Get well."

Eddy could only stare in amazement as Ben left the room. Eddy even had a few tears. "There goes a nice kid. This world needs a bunch like him because there's much work to be accomplished!"

Abaddon

The Employer of Bought Souls – Mr. A. Baddon – The Fallen Angel of the Bottomless Pit

"Beware of false prophets, which come to you in sheep's clothing, but inwardly they are ravening wolves, Ye shall know them by their fruits." Matt. 7:15.

Abaddon is the angel of the bottomless pit who appears to be a ruler of evil spirits as described in the Book of Revelation.

"And the shapes of the locusts were like unto horses prepared unto battle; and on their heads were as it were crowns like gold, and their faces were as the faces of men. And they had hair as the hair of women, and their teeth were as the teeth of lions. And they had breastplates, as it were breastplates of iron; and the sound of their wings was as the sound of chariots of many horses running to battle, and they had tails like unto scorpions, and there were stings in their tails: and their power was to hurt men five months." Rev. 9:7-10.

"And they had a king over them, which is the angel of the bottomless pit, whose name in the Hebrew tongue is Abaddon, but in the Greek tongue hath his name Apollyon." Rev. 9:11.

Abaddon

(Satan's Angel of The Bottomless Pit)

"Mr. Riffle, you have someone here to see you."

"Yea, who is it? Is it the undertaker?"

"No, not him. The person signed in as Mr. A. Baddon. Do you know him?"

"Unfortunately, he's one of my past business associates. One that I don't brag about. Besides, I thought that he was deceased. If he's able to walk upright, let him pass. If I raise my left arm, throw him out."

A. Baddon enters the room and makes his way over to Eddy. He puts his cold icy hand on his shoulder and squawks: "I bet you didn't expect to see me again in this lifetime, did you, tattletale? Well, here I am. As they say: They missed me by 'this' much! I thought that you might be joining me in the past tense and I'm sorry to see that you are still kicking. What's the matter? Has the black cat got your tongue?"

Eddy then responded to this unexpected appearance of "The Employer of Bought Souls" by brushing his hand from his shoulder: "I'm flabbergasted! I was told that you bit the dust in that Pier 5 raid by the coppers. It was out of my hands. You ain't mad at me, are you? Anyway, you look pretty awful for a walking corpse. What's with the disguise? Masquerade party? What are you here for – to pay me back?"

"No, you stool pigeon, just the opposite! Bullets won't stop me from my appointed task. I'm here to help you even if you are nothing to me but small change! Everything was going as planned and you allowed me to make the decisions but then that conscience thing got all your attention. Basically, I was doing you a favor and making you rich. Lots of money always works miracles in satisfying greedy souls and that's what I was offering. It could have been a great relationship but you faltered and ratted me out to your buddy, Sam Holler. And I'm not too happy about losing Aebra Arlington. I had her in my grasp but you turned mellow and got sympathetic and forgave her. So, what did she do? She turned me out – I lost her because of you. I bet you got a few points from upstairs on that one, as if I care!"

"But not all is lost. You still have time to join my team. Just say the word and I'll take you to great heights and power. Anyway, that bothersome Michael deceived you and stole that $15,000 check of yours! You see Eddy, some people are not what they seem. Michael is fake news. Now, take a look at me for example: I've never what I seem to be – I'm many things!"

To demonstrate, Abaddon changed his appearance to that of The Clown with her red face and black clothes: "That's right, Eddy, I had you in my sights with that M-16 but decided to let you off the hook. I'm the nice guy here. I told you that I would be back. The big boss still wants you! I'm here to let you know that you still have a choice. I will set you free to do whatever you want with all the riches and human pleasures that you could possibly desire. Michael will just tie you down with a bunch of rules and regulations. And, he's not even the top man. That Jesus fellow tells him what to do. So, come with me – sweet times await."

"Wait a minute, Mr. A. Baddon or Mr. Employer or Mr. Clown, do you think that I am confused or blind to the facts? I think that I know who you are and what you want. Get thee behind me! I don't want what you have to offer. The bottomless pit is reserved for you and your big boss – the serpent. I have been blessed with the promises and protection of The Shield."

If anything would jolt me back to life, this visit would do the trick. I closed my eyes for just a second trying to muster the nerve to reject such a powerful force. I opened my eyes and responded: "The Bible tells me that the forces of darkness cannot take rejection." But, where did he go? "Oh well, he's already disappeared. Maybe back to wherever he came from and good riddance."

Gabriel – Friar Tuck – Mr. Patron

Nurse Cranky: "Mr. Riffle, you have someone here to see you."

Mr. Patron enters the room and makes his way over to Eddy.

Eddy speaks: "Well, let's see, its Mr. Patron – the bum, or Friar Tuck, or St. Gabriel. Aw, skip it! How's old Joe doing?"

"He's a busy man. The diner is a favorite for customers that seek guidance. They just come in right off the street. Joe calls me and then feeds them until I arrive. It's a team effort. But today, I came to see you and I brought others with me; your army buddies of the past."

As if on key, edging into Eddy's view from the shadows were three undefinable spiritual forms. At first, they were not recognizable as to who or what. One by one, each began a process of forming into a creation that appeared very familiar.

Eddy rubbed his eyes in disbelief: The first was Bill – killed in action when that guard post was hit by a mortar explosion. He was dressed in his battle uniform but without injuries or trauma. He looked great!

The next spirit then began to transform; it was Gordon! Then the next; it was Dietrich! They both were dressed in their battle uniforms and without injuries – also, both KIA. The last time Eddy saw them was in a ghost nightmare; their forms were roaming the battlefields helping out buddies. They looked great!

Eddy was unable to speak and tears filled his eyes. He stood up and reached out his arms, wanting to hug them, but it was not possible. He quickly realized that they were not of human substance and sat back down. His mind was now puzzled as to what was happening and why.

Bill moved and fronted Eddy. He spoke: "It's been a long time, sergeant. It's good to see that The Deacon is making a comeback. It was too bad that he went into hiding for a spell. The last time that we were face to face, The Deacon comforted me as I was fading; preparing to fly away. Your prayer for me was powerful and almost did the trick, but it was too late; my injuries were too severe. You were my last picture. The angel that came for me was holding my head while you prayed. He could not save me but he witnessed you and Bob and your critical need. He materialized into his angel form and blessed and shielded you both."

"Thank you, Bill; that's great news. I've always hoped that it was an angel that was standing in the rubble of that guard post. And now I know why he was there. As you said, he came to collect you and take you to the place where peacemakers, the children of God, all go. He saved us from sure death by hiding us from the NVA."

"That's right. Both of you were given a reprieve. But no one lives forever, so it's time for you to be the man that you have always envisioned of yourself. I've come to remind you that you are still on orders to be a servant right here on this earth. So, dress-right-dress and snap to attention – just like old times! And remember, Sergeant Riffle, there really is that better place, just like Jesus promised. It's called New Jerusalem and when the correct time arrives, we will be made new. It's on the horizon – just in the wink of an eye!"

Eddy looking about, then spoke: "The Deacon needs his buddies this time. I must break that barrier of hurt and shame that keeps me from God. But first, I want you to pinch me so I can see if this is really happening; I'm in a coma, I think."

"Ouch! Three pinches – they are real!"

Eddy felt the need for prayer. He led them. At this precious moment, he released his self-destructive bonds, his guilt and his fear. His long-suppressed PTSD and darkness of soul has now been replaced by the blessings of Jesus; the Risen Saviour and The Shield.

After the prayer, Eddy opened his eyes to a marvelous sight; the spirit forms of Bill, Gordon and Dietrich, were all smiling. All of them were special – a band of brothers. Slowly, they began dissipating. They were called back to their posts. Someday, they will all meet again and be made new.

Eddy has been in a coma for a short time, but has experienced many revelations. He is puzzled and unable to determine which were fact and which were fantasy or dreams. Did he commit atrocious behavior? Will he have to stand before the judge and account? Will they understand or put him into an institution? Will he finally be reconciled with family? He does believe that

God's plan for him will prevail. His conscience is at peace as he quietly waits for what's next.

Before Eddy relaxed too much, the future plan for him began to unfold when his college buddy and police lieutenant, Lt. Sam Holler arrived. He possessed damaging and life altering documents that could effectively end Eddy's renewed hope. A miracle is needed to sort out this mess.

Lt. Sam Holler opens the door to Eddy's hospital room. He has an envelope in his hand. He sits down beside his friend's bed. "I wish that I didn't have to do this."

"Didn't have to do what? Oh, it's you, Sam. What's up?"

"Here, read this and then we will talk."

Subpoena

Informal Request for Appearance

Eddy Edward Riffle

Investigation into the following events:

A. *An unknown shot Mr. A. Baddon while in a police raid.*

B. *An unknown shot and wounded a person known as The Clown.*

C. *An unknown shot and killed Roddy Shaw.*

D. *Inconclusive: Detective Boone was found lying in ocean waters just off the beach and near his residence. Cause of death: drowning with possible implications.*

Cause for hearing:

A. *Mr. Eddy E. Riffle stated that he had ownership of the type of weapon used in the above violations. To wit: Army-issue M24 long distance, 800m range, rifle with scope.*

B. *Mr. Eddy E. Riffle personally interacted in some capacity with all victims listed above.*

Mr. Eddy. E. Riffle is requested to appear in the Orange County Courthouse at the specified date of two months from this date to determine degree of involvement in the above-named incidents. By Order of Judge G.R. Rule.

"This is serious, Eddy. I think that there is enough circumstantial evidence to warrant an indictment. I'll help all I can but the DA has warned me to be neutral and conduct a fair investigation. My hands are tied. Any suggestions?"

"Sam, sorry that you have to go through this trauma. All I can tell you is that I just don't remember if I did any of this stuff. You will have to find out one way or another. If I am involved, I need to pay up."

Sam got up to leave when Nurse Cranky entered the room. "Is Mr. Holler still here?"

"Yes, that would be me."

"Some man just dropped this note off and told me to give it to you."

"Thanks."

"Eddy, do you know Robert Zyler Starman?"

"That's Bob, my buddy from my Vietnam days! What is it?"

Sam read the note before responding: "Listen to this, Eddy!"

Sgt. Robert Zyler Starman

Sgt. Starman: US Army. Served with Sgt. Eddy Riffle in the 14th Artillery, Americal Division, Chu Lai, Vietnam. Received Army Commendation Medal, two Purple Hearts, Bronze Star. Honorable Discharge – 1972.

After my first tour of duty in Vietnam, I went home to my family and friends. I tried to understand the USA way of life but it was too frivolous for my state of mind. I could not adjust and was in constant trouble with the law and my family. My only choice, as I saw it, was to reenlist in the Army where I was appreciated.

A mere cannoneer of a 105 howitzer would never satisfy me because I yearned to contribute more to my country – make an impact. So, I joined the Special Forces Branch and trained as a sniper. As for me, holding someone's life in my hands is the peak of emotional resolve. Get the job done and do it for the right reasons. But I never could figure what was right and what was wrong in this line of work. At least, I was an important somebody.

After many years, my military obligation came to an end. Over time, I made many friends and they had inside contacts. They helped me to secure employment in the Secret Service. Because of my special skill, I was assigned covert operations and became known as one of the best in long-range targets. For my own safety, I went by my middle name of Zyler. When I lost my perspective, I was forced into retirement.

Not ready to hang it up, I found myself lacking in formal education and experience at real work, so I let it be known that I was available for contract work; kind of like have gun will travel. A former associate in the sniper business, became aware of my situation and vouched for me. I received a call. My services were needed by a syndicate with unscrupulous enterprises. By coincidence, this organization was having turf problems with another faction headed by Mr. A. Baddon, a.k.a. The Employer. He was taking too much and in charge of too many enterprises – not good for his health. I was highly paid to make a change. At that time, I did not know that Sgt. Eddy Riffle was involved with Mr. A. Baddon until I saw him lurking in the rafters of that hangar on Pier 5. I could hardly believe my eyes but it really was The Deacon.

I found a nice spot in the back rafters that hid me from Eddy. When the time was right and in all that confusion and noise, I completed a perfect shot. I'm not in need of credit, so I let the police congratulate themselves. But then someone had to perform an autopsy and then somebody else started scratching their head.

As for Detective Boone, I was not involved with his demise. He probably got some poetic justice.

Then this clown situation began. I was informed that The Employer was still alive and active. I could not have missed, so I have no idea how it escaped death. My sources informed me that he had taken a disguise in the form of a clown. It was hiding from a mouth-closer called Zyler. I want to make it perfectly clear that Zyler is me. I am that Zyler and being a sniper is my profession. I am after The Employer and won't rest until I mark him once and forever.

In further investigation, I discovered that my army buddy was the legal expert for a new capo – Mr. Client. I was surprised at first, but I calculated that The Deacon had fell off the church wagon. It probably was for the same reason I'm no good – PTSD. So, I decided to stay behind the scenes and help him keep out of trouble. He was just about everything for me on the battlefield and helped me through rough times. I won't forget.

It wasn't hard to start tracking Eddy. He is a big lummox when he is unsuspecting that a sniper is following him – not to hurt him but to protect him.

Who would think that Eddy could get into trouble watching a parade? That was the first time since Vietnam that I saw my friend. Hidden by a baseball cap and sunglasses, I sat at a nearby table. He could have hit me with a popcorn kernel.

The clown made him a proposal. It wanted Eddy to eliminate Zyler and get it mega cash at the same time; neat plan, but it didn't work.

After investigating the clown at my former field office, all the info that I could get confirmed was that this person was "not of this world!" I thought: "Maybe where it comes from, they have nine lives, so I will erase a few."

Staked myself out on the 12th floor of the office building, I followed the action. The only shot I could get was when Lt. Holler cuffed the clown and took it across the parking lot to the police van. I pulled the trigger and hit the clown dead center. I thought that it was a goner but somehow, it twisted and the bullet apparently missed; or did it? I can't miss two times in a row!

Feeling that I still needed to surveil Eddy, it was by accident that I crossed paths with Jonnie and Roddy Shaw at a bookie hangout. They were arguing over back loans and money owed – that kind of stuff. When I heard the name Riffle mentioned, I became alarmed. So, I asked my sources and got the inside story. I never cared for Roddy Shaw, but I do care for Eddy Riffle and now for his brother, Jonnie.

The best way to get to ground zero was to follow Roddy Shaw. I did and I saw the whole deal. He hid in that alley and was going to have an old-fashioned shootout with Jonnie. It would have been a mismatch. Roddy Shaw was adept at pistol shooting and didn't care who he shot. Jonnie had no chance. I owe Eddy too much to stand by and let his brother get ambushed. That's what happened. I nailed that bushwhacker! I know that I did not miss this time.

This is my confession about my involvement. It's in my own words and written by my own hand and by my own free will.

Sorry, Lt. Holler, I will not turn myself in to the authorities because I'm not finished with business. I know that I'm lost to the darkness and probably to the bottomless pit, but I plan on setting things right until that day arrives. If I can find The Shield, who knows? Besides, my buddy, Sgt. Eddy Riffle, will help me – he's The Deacon!

Sam to Eddy: "Here it is; your exoneration. All charges will be dropped. But that is not the good news. Your brother, Jonnie, is alive and well. He's been helping us on the investigation. We had to smoke out the sniper. All the evidence was pointing at you and we had to act. Jonnie really didn't want to go along with that story about him floating in the bay, but I convinced him that it was all for your good."

"The department knew right off that Jonnie did not shoot Robby Shaw and it was the sniper that pulled the trigger. Besides, with that football injury, he's such an awful shot that he blasted that bakery in the butt. If the sniper had not made the hit, Jonnie would have been a goner."

"One thing more: sorry, but we did not figure on you getting attacked by those henchmen. We really messed up there and you had to pay for it. Jonnie was out of his mind until you bucked up and started fussing with Nurse Cranky. And, since we were shooting blanks, the DA had no choice but to charge you with the murder of Roddy Shaw. It's a good thing that your pal, Bob Zyler, has now confessed and this puts the icing on the cake. I just wish I could take a piece of that cake and let the DA have it on the snout!"

"Thanks Sam; you the man!"

Chapter Twenty
St. Michael Returns – The Verdict

"A just weight and balance are the Lord's: all the weights of the bag are his work." Prov. 16:11.

The room was unusually quiet and dark. Visitors and visions had subsided. Family will arrive later. Nurse Cranky, real or unreal, was taking a break. She wanted her patient to get some rest. She had opened the window so he could get some fresh air. He had been very busy while being in a coma.

A gentle breeze that had filled the room with comforting caresses, was now becoming agitated with bluster. Curtains and shades began flapping to and fro. An eeriness crept into the room. Darkness was interrupted by quick flashes of light. An apparition was present. Its personality blossomed like sweet Lilac, which permeated the sleeping patient.

All in one: The Grim Reaper, The good Angel of Death, The Guardian of the Church, and The Archangel – St. Michael materialized from his special viewing spot: he watched the whole show! And, now It was time for The Verdict!

The hooded angel eased his way out of the shadows. His presence was intimidating as he hovered slightly above ground with sickle in one hand, sword in his belt, and the balancing scales in the other hand; that's his 'I mean business' attire. He floated above the peaceful target before settling beside the bed. He changed his appearance into the same form that Eddy envisioned on their first visit. He spoke in clear voice; one that Eddy would remember and not become alarmed. "So, they call you Eddy!"

Gently opening his eyes: "Yea, who is it? Are you bringing me flowers and sweet grapes or is that a whipping stick that's ready to harvest the chaff? I know who you are even if I am groggy. Michael, did you ride in on your black horse?"

Eddy was calm, laughed and continued: "Good thing that Nurse Cranky did not get a clear look at you or she would still be beating you with that leather belt that she carries. She uses it on unruly patients or anybody else that might get in her way.

Michael speaks: By the way, I know Nurse Cranky very well; we work together; it's one of my often-used disguises to get inside information."

The sick man: I thought that she looked familiar but a little homely for an angel.

"Eddy, Eddy, you amaze me. Lying here with very little of your own blood left in your body, you're still able to find something funny. How about if I make you a promise. If we wind up flying away, I will let you ride up front on that black horse; whether it's up or we go down. We do have a heat buffer."

"Thanks Mike. Riding your horse going upward is preferred. But I hope that I'm not done on this earth. I want to go home to my family. I should leave right now, even in this chilly gown. All I really need is my toothbrush and eyebrow tweezers. You can collect me at a later date. You don't mind if I call you Mike, do you? I've become close to you lately. If you like, it'll be St. Mike!"

"Sure, whatever, but I still have my job to do. I treat every soul with care and respect. We know that it's not easy for anyone to live four score years in this dangerous world. I'm not the meanie that everyone is so scared to meet. I've been around a long time and helped many to find their way home. And, what I have found is that most are ready and relieved that their tribulations are over; it's the promise of salvation through Jesus and that joy cometh in the morning. When the time arrives, it's likened to a woman giving birth: 'A woman when she is in travail hath sorrow, because her hour is come: but as soon as she is delivered of the child, she remembereth no more the anguish, for joy that a man is born into the world.'" John 16:21

"Well, Mike, I'll have to admit that you are a hard angel for us mortals to understand. I guess all our questions will be answered; when the time is right. Say, one more thing. I'm sorry for that wrestling match we had on Easter. Remember, I jumped out of darkness and right on top of your back. What a match! I should have known that you are a square guy."

Interruption: Ellie, Lynn, Niki, Jamie, and Aaron pushed opened the door to the room. "We have the release papers. It's time to go home. We're going to have an ice cream and cake celebration." Catching a glimpse of Michael as he slithered back into the shadows, Ellie shrieked: "What was that; a ghost?"

Michael quickly stepped back into the light. This time he presented a kind face and not so much like Eddy. He said: "So, they call you Eddy's family!"

Eddy could see the fright of his family and intervened: "Michael, they came to get me. You can't stop them; they've got their minds made up. I was almost on my way and I've already packed that tweezer and toothbrush. I'm not too selfish to want to go home, am I Mike?"

Michael smiled: "Having a loving family is tops and is a blessing that all should recognize; it's part of God's plan. I sense that your family is still a little upset at my sudden appearance and do not understand what's occurring."

Gently, he removed his golden themed headwear revealing to all an "aura" of light.

"This light is called a halo and God gave me this to reveal that I am truly one of His select. It's time for an angelic presence right here on this earth and that's why I'm here. We are like a life preserver to those who have fallen overboard and will perish without a simple lift to give them buoyance. So, don't be afraid, I'm here with God's countenance."

Eddy summoning his courage: "Do I have a chance or is it curtains?"

Ellie: "Are you here to take Eddy to heaven?"

"Let's just see about that. Normally, I do not include the whole family for The Verdict, but there is always a first time. So, try not to be too excited or scared; it's something all must face. God is love and He understands your fears. That's why Jesus was endowed with a human body – incarnate. That way, God knows all your wants and feelings."

St. Michael calmly reached under his cape and retrieved his scales and set them on the table. He retrieved his sickle and sword and stood them against the wall; waved his hand and they disappeared. Closing his eyes, he lifted another object from under his cape. It had the form of gases that was illumined with colors of the rainbow signifying God's covenant with mankind. "And the bow shall be in the cloud; and I will look upon it, that I may remember the everlasting covenant between God and every living creature of all flesh that is upon the earth."

He placed the rainbow vision on a pivot point of those weighing scales. The entire Riffle family sat hypnotized by its glowing beauty; not sure of what they were witnessing. Eddy knew that everything he had done in his life would be "weighed on the scales" and that this Holy image would now render a verdict.

All watched in wonderment. To the eyes of beholders, the images were similar to the visualization of objects within white fluffy clouds and how those objects can slowly reshape and change into new objects and delight imaginations within their own perceptions.

Spoken words came forth from out of the ever-changing haze – endearing, soft, and piercing:

"For God so loved the world, that he gave His only begotten Son, that whosoever believeth in Him should not perish, but have everlasting life."

"A prodigal son has returned – follow Me into the great tribulations."

"And Jesus walking by the sea of Galilee, saw two brethren, Simon called Peter, and Andrew his brother, casting a net into the sea: for they were fishers. And he saith unto them, "Follow me, and I will make you Fishers of Men." It's time; The nets are once again empty!"

The Verdict – "Follow Me"

"Follow Me – the sealing of the saints is yet to occur. The casting of the nets lies just ahead as mankind evolves into the beginning of woes and the great tribulations and the fulfillment of Biblical prophesies: 'And I heard the number of them which were sealed: and there were sealed a hundred and forty and four thousand of all the tribes of Israel.'" Rev 7:1-4

It is believed by some religions that the sealing of the 144,000 are high priests, ordained unto the holy order of God, to administer the everlasting gospel; for they are they who are ordained out of every nation, kindred, tongue, and people, by the angels to whom is given power over the nations of the earth, to bring as many as will come to the church of the Firstborn.

"Is it possible that Eddy Riffle, so lost, so confused, and so like a vessel that was broken beyond repair, be delivered into the steadfastness of a saint; one of the 144,000? Why not you?" The Son of God came to save that which was lost. Luke 19:10

St. Michael mounted his snorting black horse that eagerly flapped his giant wings because it was time to go home; the comfort of the corral was calling. Up and on and away; into the heavens they flew.

One might ask: "Why was the archangel so concerned with an insignificant soul such as Eddy Riffle?" The answer: "Because that's what St. Michael does.

He's the guardian of The Church of The Firstborn and there is much in the tribulations to be accomplished: 'yet there is a little season ahead, until fellow servants and their brethren, should they be killed as they were, should be fulfilled.' Saints will still be under constant attack, especially during the times of woe that are prophesied."

St. Michael helped Daniel in the lion's den: Then said he unto me, Fear not, Daniel: for from the first day that thou didst set thine heart to understand, and to chasten thyself before thy God, thy words were heard, and I have come for thy word. Lo, Michael, one of the chief princes, came to help me. Daniel 10: 8-13

Daniel said: My God hath sent his angel, and hath shut the lions' mouth, that they have not hurt me – Dan. 6:22

What about the Riffles? What should they do? Eddy grabbed the discharge paperwork and looked at his stunned family. He winked. It was the signal and they all bolted for the door – they were going home together – get out before somebody changes their mind! But just before the door shut behind them, Eddy superstitiously glanced backward to see if any lingering angels might be sneaking about. His eye was attracted to something lying on the table. It was a plain document but it still seemed out of place. Eddy rushed and grabbed it and hurriedly opened the flap. "Hey, wait a minute, it's my missing check!"

A note: "Not all of your experiences were by divine inspiration; some were within your free-will; others had a little help. Mysterious ways – which ones? Don't worry, the check won't bounce, if you hurry!"

Eddy Edward Riffle recovered from this latest near-death experience and remained in Orlando, Florida with his family. He took up the mantle of a Fisher of Men, but had to retire from operations and let the younger kids run things. He became immobile due to illnesses associated with "Agent Orange" exposure while serving (boots on the ground) in Vietnam. A senseless tragedy was finally recognized. The Agent Orange Act of 1991 directed the Veterans Administration to provide benefits and treatment of afflictions caused by toxic herbicide exposure. At least a dozen illnesses are attributed to Agent Orange and automatically qualify for benefits.

Grandsons, Jamie and Aaron, completed their education. Granddad saw to it because that was always his plan. He loved them. He also gave them direction: "All my life, I have struggled with trying to figure out what is right and what is wrong. When you have an urge and are faced with that decision, remember these six words; "well done good and faithful servant." If you can't answer "yes" to that judgement then examine your conscious. Then in quiet, listen for guidance; it's the place only known to oneself; if you chose wrongly and in defiance, you will soon know."

Both of the boys have escaped effects from Agent Orange, so far. They became attorneys-at-law and private detectives; their heritage. It's in their blood. They want to become deacons in their local Christian church. They have assumed their grandfather's stuffy office and lousy broken-down rocking chair, but it's too risky to take a seat.

Alpha and Omega – The Beginning and The End

One Hand Held the Bible; One hand held the Gun

All my life I have worried; what's right and what's wrong.
Not seeing what's beside me; He was there all along.
One hand held the Bible; one hand held the Gun.
One hand saves the lost; while the other pays a cost.

Why am I forsaken? Nightmares run free.
In the depths of darkness; with no light to see.
Harshness of war; brought trauma and pain.
Many soldiers left helpless; many lives left with stain.

Many roads I have traveled; many reasons to worry.
Long nights filled with stress; morning light won't hurry.
My face is now wrinkled; with age and sorrow.
Enough hurt for today; can't count on tomorrow.

Many sins I've committed; like grains of the sands.
Cleansed by blood; my life's in His hands.
All my life I have worried; what's right and what's wrong.
Not seeing what's beside me; God was there all along.

The archangel St. Michael; he planted a seed.
And gave me wisdom; in God's Holy seed.
In my soul is The Deacon; forged by The Shield.
Faith and family; all I did was to yield.

The Deacon now chooses; which life he will follow.
One blessed with love; or one filled with hollow.
Named in God's book; that He holds in His hands.
Cleansed by blood; I live by His plans.

With both hands I hold the Bible; the gun has been tossed.
I no longer worry; Jesus paid the cost.
In my soul is The Deacon; forged by The Shield.
Faith and family; all I did was to yield.

By: John E. Howard

The Deacon's Homily

Events that create PTSD seem to take center stage as one ages and invite disbelief and uncertainty. Will I or won't I have my name etched in the Book of Life and allowed into New Jerusalem? Eddy Riffle fought the good fight and gained peace by finding faith in the promises of Jesus – The Shield.

Rest assured:

Because he hath appointed a day, in the which he will judge the world in righteousness by that man whom he hath ordained; whereof he hath given "assurance unto all men," in that he hath raised him (Jesus) from the dead. Book of Acts.

"The Shield" is available and calling to all – seek, discover, believe, understand, and sanctify.

Seek: In times like these, we need a saviour. Come to terms with yourself that indeed there is a saviour who welcomes all who seek with open arms.

Discover: Attend the gatherings of those with like precious faith who study the Holy Scriptures as written within the Bible. Join in the teachings and discussions – learn and discover the identity of the saviour.

Believe: God speaks – I will not open the windows of heaven and send down a blessing if there is not room in your heart to receive it. Make room in your heart for the saviour and believe what he has promised.

Understand: Be still and know. It's simply finding true faith that the saviour is Jesus: He was tortured and died on the cross for the forgiveness of sins and for mankind's eternal salvation. He was buried in the tomb. He was resurrected. He appeared unto His following before His ascension unto His Holy Father in Heaven. By His example, He proved that there is life after death and that The Holy Scriptures are written by The Holy Spirit and are The Words of God. He promises that there is a better place that awaits us all and someday He will come again.

Sanctifying by water: One Lord, one faith, one baptism. Eph 4:5

Put off the natural man and becometh a saint through the atonement of Christ the Lord, and becometh as a child, submissive, meek, humble, patient, full of love, willing to submit to all things which the Lord seeth fit to inflict upon him, even as a child doth submit to his father. "Mosiah 3"

For all that suffer with PTSD, may you find peace of mind by finding The Shield; The Son of God, Jesus Christ. It is hoped that through this story and by His truths and promises, one can come to realize that Jesus saves. Start finding Him today.

Amen, and may God bless and keep us until we meet again.

John E. Howard

The following section contains the authors reference material and his impression and beliefs about The Next Word.

Prophesied beginning of woes – birth pains
The basic of a book sequel titled The Next Word
Fishers of Men
Author's reference material – information on angels, The Rapture, The Seven Seals

From the author: An interpretation

Prophesied Beginning of Woes – Birth Pains

Presently on earth, the Holy Scriptures and Christian values are experiencing increased criticism, suppression, and discrimination. And as a result, many have weakened and allowed themselves to fall in line and become permissive and lukewarm.

The battle for souls between the Archangel, St. Michael – the leader of heaven's angels, and Abaddon – the leader of Satan's band of fallen angels, has intensified to the point that an Earthly presence is manifested.

The diminishing of Christianity as foretold in the Holy Scriptures appears to have arrived. Churches, synagogues, houses of worship and children's schools at all levels, are under siege by crazed martyr-seekers resulting in destruction of property, the taking of innocent lives, and leaving survivors scarred for life both physically and mentally. In addition, many souls are hypnotized into abandoning their faith completely, as evidenced by open pronouncement of love of self with claims of entitlement due to victim-hood. Consequently, these actions have paved the way for disrespect for the constitutional laws of the land and the basic rights of others. Out of fear, armed protection has become necessary for the everyday citizen just to walk the streets – conceal and carry – stand your ground.

Mankind has generally become ignorant of the obvious and deny fulfillment of Biblical prophesies. As foretold, on the four corners of earth, global warming, fierce storms with floods, hurricanes, earthquakes, forest fires, volcanic eruptions, and new strains of virus and plague have wreaked havoc and left many deaths in their wake. Economically, the gap between the have and the have-nots has reached epidemic proportion and thereby created an atmosphere of friction and hatred leaving many homeless and destitute. Riots and lawlessness in the streets abound pitting citizen vs citizen!

For every kind of beasts, and of birds, and of serpents, and of things in the sea, is tamed, and hath been tamed of mankind: But the tongue can no man tame; it is an unruly evil, full of deadly poison. James 3

The graying of America is currently projected to slow religious growth over the next few decades as younger generations show less interest in religious life. The number of Christians is estimated to decline from three-quarters of the world's population in 2010 to two-thirds by the year 2050. "Florida, The Daily Sun article dated 9-23-19."

Failure to heed: "I know thy works, that thou art neither cold nor hot: I would thou wert cold or hot. So then because thou art lukewarm, and neither cold nor hot I will spue thee out of my mouth." Rev 3:15-1

The Next Word

The Association with Lt. Holler, Judge Rule, Aebra Arlington, the Riffle family, and Sgt. Robert Zyler Starman, go forth into the great tribulations and will experience many exciting tales that will be told. They are joined by Triple AAA—Aebra Arlington; an expert constitutional lawyer.

Jamie and Aaron Riffle follow in their grandfather's footsteps. As attorneys and private detectives, they help victims of suppression and discrimination that are hunted and harassed because of their beliefs in Christianity. In retaliation, the forces of the opposing factions have taken hostages and make demands. The fathers, Isaac and Eli, being trained soldiers will seek to free the incarcerated.

The ageless sniper, Zyler, remains undercover and continues his rogue attacks on evil perpetrators while stalking the fallen angel of the bottomless pit, Abaddon. He continues his personal struggle to seek, discover, believe and understand The Shield.

Lt. Holler and Judge G. R. Rule defend the rule of law against ruthless violators that prey on the weak and defenseless. The constitution of The United States is threatened with open non-compliance with citizen riots and destruction of properties. Corruption runs rampant with love of self and great wealth and power as the motive.

Daughters, Lynn and Niki, provide the technical support and computer expertise. They control drones that scour the earth monitoring the activity of the opposition and to find the location of prison camps.

Eddy Riffle becomes a sage; a very wise man with angelic connections and visions. He leads the team toward the completion of the mission – Fisher of Men. They will face great dangers. The mission: Save as many as will come to the Church of the Firstborn. Eddy Riffle awaits the totality of being sealed with the 144,000. It could mean his ultimate sacrifice!

Opposing factions gain control and deceive the masses:

"Behold, I send you forth as sheep in the midst of wolves: be ye therefore wise as serpents, and harmless as doves." Matt. 10:16

"Then shall they deliver you up to be afflicted, and shall kill you: and ye shall be hated of all nations for my name's sake. And then shall many be offended, and shall betray one another, and shall hate one another. And many false prophets shall rise, and shall deceive many. And because iniquity shall abound, the love of many shall wax cold. But he that shall endure unto the end, the same shall be saved. And this gospel of the kingdom shall be preached in all the world for a witness unto all nations; and then shall the end come." Matt: 24:9-14

"Now we exhort you, brethren, warn them that are unruly, comfort the feebleminded, support the weak, be patient toward all men. See that none render evil for evil unto any man; but ever follow that which is good, both among yourselves, and to all men. Rejoice evermore. Pray without ceasing. In every thing give thanks: for this is the will of God in Christ Jesus concerning you. Quench not the Spirit. Despise not prophesyings. Prove all things; hold fast that which is good. Abstain from all appearance of evil. And the very God of peace sanctify you wholly; and I pray God your whole spirit and soul and body be preserved blameless unto the coming of our Lord Jesus Christ." I Thess. 5:14-23

"But as the days of Noah were, so shall also the coming of the Son of Man be."

Sealing of the 144,000.

Hurt not the earth, neither the sea, nor the trees, till we have sealed the servants of God in their foreheads. And I heard the number of them which were sealed: and there were sealed an hundred and forty and four thousand of all the tribes of Israel. Rev 7:1-4

"And there was a war in heaven: Michael and his angels fought against the dragon; and the dragon fought and his angels, And prevailed not; neither was their place found any more in heaven. And the great dragon was cast out, that old serpent, called the Devil, and Satan, which deceiveth the whole world: he was cast out into the earth, and his angels were cast out with him." Rev. 12:7-9.

His Face in The Cloud – "Woe to the inhabitants of the earth and of the sea! for the devil is come down unto you, having great wrath, because he knoweth that he hath but a short time." Rev. 12:12.

P.S. –The end is not yet – so be it.

Married, Father, And Grandfather.

Education includes an Associates in Arts Degree in Higher Accounting – Business College, Dayton, Ohio. Further educated at Wright State University, Fairborn, Ohio.

Employed by Delco Moraine, Dayton, Ohio – a division of General Motors – 34 years – Financial/Accounting – now retired.

Vietnam veteran with 12 months in-country service – 14th Artillery. Chu Lai, Northern Vietnam – 1967-68 – earned U.S. Army Commendation Medal for meritorious service.

Self-published one book: *Faces of Grandfather* – sold on Amazon and Barnes & Noble. Released in 2007 CY.

Current endeavor: "Aspiring author of religious books."

Why? The Holy Bible states: "Forsake not the prophesies – I believe that mankind has done just that by ignoring the obvious signs!"

"That we henceforth be no more children, tossed to and fro, and carried about with every wind of doctrine, by the sleight of men, and cunning craftiness, whereby they lie in wait to deceive." Eph. 4:14.

Ordained deacon by the laying on of hands by the Elders, First Church of Christ.

John E. Howard

Fishers of Men

"What to Expect"

"Behold, I send you forth as sheep in the midst of wolves: be ye therefore wise as serpents, and harmless as doves." Matt. 10:16.

"Then shall they deliver you up to be afflicted, and shall kill you: and ye shall be hated of all nations for my name's sake. And then shall many be offended, and shall betray one another, and shall hate one another. And many false prophets shall rise, and shall deceive many. And because iniquity shall abound, the love of many shall wax cold. But he that shall endure unto the end, the same shall be saved. And this gospel of the kingdom shall be preached in all the world for a witness unto all nations; and then shall the end come." Matt: 24:9-14.

"Now we exhort you, brethren, warn them that are unruly, comfort the feebleminded, support the weak, be patient toward all men. See that none render evil for evil unto any man; but ever follow that which is good, both among yourselves, and to all men. Rejoice evermore. Pray without ceasing. In everything give thanks: for this is the will of God in Christ Jesus concerning you. Quench not the Spirit. Despise not prophesyings. Prove all things; hold fast that which is good. Abstain from all appearance of evil. And the very God of peace sanctify you wholly; and I pray God your whole spirit and soul and body be preserved blameless unto the coming of our Lord Jesus Christ." I Thess. 5:14-23.

Angel Gabriel

Gabriel means "man of God." He is the most well-known named angel to appear in Scripture. Each time he is mentioned, we see him act as a messenger to impart wisdom or a special announcement from God.

"And the angel answering said unto him, I am Gabriel, that stand in the presence of God; and am sent to speak unto thee, and to shew thee these glad tidings." St. Luke 1:19.

"And in the sixth month the angel Gabriel was sent from God unto a city of Galilee, named Nazareth, To a virgin espoused to a man whose name was Joseph, of the house of David; and the virgin's name was Mary. And the angel came in unto her, and said, Hail, thou that art highly favored, the Lord is with thee: blessed art thou among women." St. Luke 1:26-28.

Archangel Michael

Michael means "who is like God." He appears to be the one to do battle against Satan and his band of fallen angels. Michael was chosen to be the chief of all angels and called an Archangel. Archangel Michael, also known as the good Angel of Death, also known as the Grim Reaper, is frequently thought to be a personified force, due to the prominent place in human culture. Some religions in the world believe that Michael causes people's death by coming to collect them and carries their soul to Heaven. Also, in the Roman Catholic teachings, Saint Michael has four main roles. His first role is as the leader of the Army of God and the leader of heaven's forces in their triumph over the powers of hell.

The second and third roles of Michael deals with death. In his second role, he descends at the hour of death, and gives each soul the chance to redeem itself before passing; thus, consternating the devil and his minions. In his third role, he weighs souls in his perfectly balanced scales.

In his fourth role, Michael is also the guardian of the church.

"And when he had opened the third seal, I heard the third beast say, Come and see. And I beheld, and lo a black horse; and he that sat upon him had a pair of balances in his hand." Rev 6:5.

Abaddon, Apollyon

Abaddon is the angel of the bottomless pit who appears to be a ruler of evil spirits as described in the book of Revelation.

"And the shapes of the locusts were like unto horses prepared unto battle; and on their heads were as it were crowns like gold, and their faces were as the faces of men. And they had hair as the hair of women, and their teeth were as the teeth of lions. And they had breastplates, as it were breastplates of iron; and the sound of their wings was as the sound of chariots of many horses running to battle, and they had tails like unto scorpions, and there were stings in their tails: and their power was to hurt men five months." Rev. 9:7-10.

"And they had a king over them, which is the angel of the bottomless pit, whose name in the Hebrew tongue is Abaddon, but in the Greek tongue hath his name Apollyon." Rev. 9:11.

Some Angels Have Wings and Fly:

"Above it stood the seraphims: each one had six wings; with twain he covered his face, and with twain he covered his feet, and with twain he did fly." Isaiah 6:2.

Angels Can Take on the Appearance of Men:

"Be not forgetful to entertain strangers: for thereby some have entertained angels unawares." Heb. 13:2.

"And, behold, there was a great earthquake: for the angel of the Lord descended from heaven, and came and rolled back the stone from the door, and sat upon it. His countenance was like lightning, and his raiment white as snow." St Matthew 28:2-3.

The Number of Angels in Heaven:

"And I beheld, and I heard the voice of many angels round about the throne and the beasts and the elders: and the number of them was ten thousand times ten thousand, and thousands of thousands." Rev. 5-11.

$(10,000 \times 10,000 = 100 \text{ million}) + 1000s \text{ of } 1000s$ or too many to count!

The Rapture

The "rapture" is believed by many to be a transformation or the act of catching up of all Christians, dead or alive, to meet Christ in the air. It is thought to be secret and it will be unknown to the world of unbelievers at the time of its happening. The purpose of the rapture is to remove all righteous believers from the earth before or during the beginning time of God's wrath toward earth – which is called the "tribulation." Once the Church has been gathered, Satan will be turned loose upon the earth.

For the Lord himself shall descend from heaven with a shout, with the voice of the archangel, and with the trump of God: and the dead in Christ shall rise first: Then we which are alive and remain shall be caught up together with them in the clouds to meet the Lord in the air: and so shall we ever be with the Lord. Wherefore comfort one another with these words. I Thess. 4:16-18

Then shall two be in the field; the one shall be taken, and the other left. Two women shall be grinding at the mill; the one shall be taken, and the other left. Watch therefore: for ye know not what hour your Lord doth come. Matt 24: 40-42

"This know also, that in the last days perilous times shall come. For men shall be lovers of their own selves, covetous, boasters, proud, blasphemers, disobedient to parents, unthankful, unholy. Without natural affection, trucebreakers, false accusers, incontinent, fierce, despisers of those that are good, traitors, heady, high-minded, lovers of pleasures more than lovers of God; Having a form of godliness, but denying the power thereof." 11Tim. 3:1-5

"Above all, taking the shield of faith, wherewith ye shall be able to quench all the fiery darts of the wicked." Eph 6:16

The Seven Seals

Revelations 6: 1-2: "First Seal: And I saw when the Lamb opened one of the seals, and I heard, as it were the noise of thunder, one of the four beasts saying, Come and see. And I saw, and behold a white horse: and he that sat on him had a bow; and a crown was given unto him: and he went forth conquering, and to conquer."

Revelations 6: 3-4: "And when he had opened the second seal, I heard the second beast say, Come and see. And there went out another horse that was red: and power was given to him that sat thereon to take peace from the earth, and that they should kill one another: and there was given unto him a great sword."

Revelations 6: 5-6: "And when he had opened the third seal, I heard the third beast say, Come and see. And I beheld, and lo a black horse; and he that sat upon him had a pair of balances in his hand. And I heard a voice in the midst of the four beasts say, A measure of wheat for a penny, and three measures of barley for a penny; and see thou hurt not the oil and the wine."

Revelations 6: 7-8: "And when he had opened the fourth seal, I heard the fourth beast say, Come and see. And I looked, and behold a pale horse: and his name that sat on him was Death, and Hell followed with him. And Power was given unto them over the fourth part of the earth, to kill with sword, and with hunger, and with death, and with the beast of the earth."

Revelations 6: 9-11: "And when he had opened the fifth seal, I saw under the altar the souls of them that were slain for the word of God, and for the testimony that they held: And they cried with a loud voice, saying, How long, O Lord, holy and true, dost thou not judge and avenge our blood on them that dwell on the earth? And white robes were given unto every one of them; and it was said unto them, that they should rest for yet a little season, until their fellow servants also and their brethren, should they be killed as they were, should be fulfilled."

Revelations 6: 12-17: "And I beheld when he had opened the sixth seal, and, lo, there was a great earthquake; and the sun became black as sackcloth of hair, and the moon became as blood; And the stars of heaven fell unto the earth, even as a fig tree casteth her untimely figs, when she is shaken of a mighty wind. And the heavens departed as a scroll when it is rolled together; and every mountain and island were moved out of their places. And the kings of the earth and the great men, and the rich men, and the chief captains, and the mighty men, and every bondman, and every free man, hid themselves in the dens and in the rocks of the mountains; And said to the mountains and rocks, Fall on us, and hide us from the face of him that sitteth on the throne, and from the wrath of the Lamb: For the great day of wrath is come and who shall be able to stand?"

Revelations 8: 1-2: "And when he had opened the seventh seal, there was silence in heaven about the space of half an hour. And I saw the seven angels which stood before God; and to them were given seven trumpets." Revelations 8, 9, 10 (the sounding of the seven trumpets).